# Crimson King

# J.B. Rockwell

ISBN: 978-1-950305-71-1 (sc)
ISBN: 978-1-950305-72-8 (ebook)

First printing edition: October 29, 2021
Published by Bizarro Pulp Press in the United States of America.
Cover Design by Nicholas Day | Layout by Don Noble
Proofreading and Interior Layout by Scarlett R. Algee
Edited by Nicholas Day

Bizarro Pulp Press, an imprint of JournalStone Publishing
3052 Sassafras Trail
Carbondale, Illinois 62901


Bizarro Pulp Press may be ordered through booksellers or by contacting:
JournalStone | www.journalstone.com

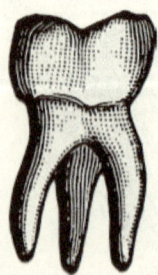

On a brittle night, I birthed the Bimiangus.
In a brittle house, perched on a brittle cliff.
A monster that rumbled and rambled about my head,
Tearing at tethers and kicking down walls.

Feasting, always feasting on the corruption I held,
The rotted carcasses and plague-bearing rats.
Fatted and swollen, he clawed his way out,
Stretching and straining to escape my embrace.

And claim the world, the entire world,
Everything in it, and everything I was.
He stole from me, shamelessly, every last drop,
Horrid and heinous in his suckling at blood,
Gnawing the tattered, tender flesh from my body.

Wanting, always wanting and arguing for more,
Unceasing in his hunger for death.
For months, I drifted in a shattered state,
Vacillating between horror and joy,
Helpless and hopeless and frozen to the bone,
Until the queerest thing happened and I woke.

In that desperate, delirious, haze-shaded space,
I found a fondness for my terrible-toothed child.
All the fear, all the hatred, it melted away.
I grew to love the Bimiangus, in that moment.
Protective of the bull I'd birthed from my head.

You'll see.
You'll understand yourself, one day.
He'll come for you, my Bimiangus.
He'll come for you, and he'll eat you too.

# Crimson King

# ONE

THE FIRST THING Casey noticed was the heat—a blast furnace that hit him as he opened the door. Not the sandblast heat of summer in the desert, more of a slow-rolling swamp roast typical of this part of upstate New York.

The second thing was that cow in Mr. Perkins' pasture. The weird one that showed up a few days ago. The one that looked nothing at all like any of the *other* cows in that field.

"*Moo!*" it lowed, long tongue flickering, slimy strings of saliva coating its chest.

"Ew. Gross."

"What's the matter?" Nana's gnarled fingers settled on Casey's shoulders as she joined him by the door. "Whatcha see out there?"

"Cow." Casey flapped a hand at the bovine in question. "Looks funny."

"That's not a cow, honey. It's a bull. See?" Nana pointed an arthritic finger at the bovine's hind end, and the rather large, rather pendulous set of balls dangling between its legs. "Cows have udders. Bulls have a penis and testes."

"Nana!" Casey dropped his eyes, face flaming bright red.

Grandmothers weren't even supposed to *know* those words, much less actually *say* them. Then again, Nana wasn't like other grandmothers, with their doughy bodies and paper-thin skin. Fingers always pinching at cheeks. Life on the farm left Nana tough and stringy—a sunbaked old bird with iron-grey hair worn in a long, thick plait.

"Big one, I'll give you that," she said.

Casey blushed even brighter, hoping she meant the bull, not its wang.

"Damned nuisance, is what it is." Pop-Pop glanced up from his paper, glaring at the bull outside.

Like Nana, he was old and grey—thick as a brick and twice as hard. Wrinkled face tanned like leather, hair buzzed into a military style flat-top—sharp-edged and square.

"Damned thing keeps leanin' on the fence posts, stretchin' that barbed wire out. It's a wonder the whole thing hasn't come down."

Downed fences on a farm meant chaos. Livestock everywhere. Cattle eating Nana's petunias, clomping around Pop-Pop's carefully maintained yard.

Luckily, they had Casey—at least for the summer: a ten-year-old grandson available for miscellaneous chores. Like helping cranky, old Mr. Perkins—well known for his dislike of children—straighten up the posts on his barbed-wire fence.

"Ya head on over there, Casey, and help Mr. Perkins out." Pop-Pop fluffed his paper, sipping coffee in the kitchen's heat. No air conditioning anywhere in his grandparent's little farmhouse, just a fleet of fans that mostly moved the dust and warmth around.

"Do I *hafta*?" Casey whined.

"Promised him ya would. Jim ain't got no wife to take care of him—least not anymore—and no kids to help out. Farm's small, but keepin' it up's still a lotta work for one man. And that damned bull of his ain't helpin'."

The 'damned bull' *lowed* loudly, complaining voice drifting through the open door.

"Hop to," Pop-Pop told him, flicking a crooked finger.

"Yes, sir," Casey sighed, pushing the screen door open, slouching down the steps to the green, grass yard outside.

"*Moo-haroo!*" the bull greeted him, sounding surprisingly chipper for six-thirty in the morning.

"Stupid cow," Casey muttered, sulking still, wanting nothing to do with Mr. Perkins, his bull or that fence. "This is all your fault, ya know."

The bull *mooed* in confusion, blinking a few times. Cocked its head and studied Casey like some interesting bug.

Not the kind of inspection you'd *typically* expect from a cow—bull, whatever—which gave Casey pause. But he chocked it up to boredom—cattle *did* get bored, didn't they, standing around all day in the sun?—and ignored it. Shoved his hands in his pockets and scuffed his way along the grass strip separating the rutted, dirt track of Nana and Pop-Pop's driveway from the crisp whiteness of their carefully maintained board fence. That stupid bull following him, *clomp-clomp-clomping* along the long line of barbed wire and fence posts on the other side of Pop-Pop's barn board construction.

Glanced at it now and then, annoyed by its presence, wanting it to go away. Realized Nana was right—the bull *and* its wang seemed inordinately large. Much bigger than any of the cows in the pasture with it—tall, and wide, and doubled up on muscle. Shoulders bunched up like bunches of broccoli, neck a thickly corded stalk of lashed together tree limbs supporting a vast boulder of a head.

Yellow-white horns sticking like pitchforks from either side. Red fur covering the lot of it. Blood-red, *red*-red, not rust-red or red-brown. And that long tongue, flickering. Slimy, pink length trying to lick Casey like a lollypop from afar.

Casey shivered, goosebumps joining the sweat prickles coating his overheated skin. Picked up his feet, moving faster, heading for the double gate—one on the board side, second on the barbed-wire side— halfway down that stretching line of fence.

Glanced over his shoulder and found that damned bull keeping pace with him. Dogging his heels. Bovine shadow stretching long and thin, turned spindly and sinister by the early morning sun.

And the smell of it...

Not the grass and poo he associated with cattle. This one stank to high heaven. Reeked of trash and spoiled food with a hint of roadkill mixed in. A smell that *thickened*. Growing stronger as the mercury rose.

"Ugh," Casey said, plugging his nose. "You are one *disgusting* cow."

Bull. Whatever.

He hurried the rest of the way to the gate, rutted driveway continuing on to the equally rutted county road a quarter mile down. Lifted the latch on the board side gate and stepped through to a grassy demilitarized zone separating the two properties. Stopped dead at the second gate, coming face-to-face with Mr. Perkins' bull and its awful, awful stink.

"Yo, Stinky. Back up the truck."

The bull *mooed*, sidling closer, bumping into the barbed wire gate.

Looking impossibly huge now. A monumental edifice of fetid, bovine meat.

Scared him a little, looking at it. Thinking of all that muscle ranged against him. Trampling him under those wickedly cloven hoofs. And that smell. That dead 'possum stink.

Didn't want it anywhere near him—that bull *or* its stink. Took everything he had *in* him to approach that gate, with Mr. Perkins' stud guarding the other side of the fence.

"Move," he ordered, but the bull just puffed out its sides and blew. "Move, you stupid thing! Go that way!" he yelled, flailing his hands at the acres of pasturage. Swathes of green-green grass stretching behind it for days.

The bull *huffed*, snot spraying from its nostrils. Raised a cloven hoof and stomped it hard against the ground.

Not moving, clearly. Disgruntled that Casey had even asked.

"Dammit, bull. Stop being so stubborn."

The bull flicked its tongue, licking at its nose. Stretched its neck, chest pressing against the barbed wire, oblivious to the sharp points digging into its skin. "*Moo-haroo!*" it called in its yodeling voice. Glassy eyes glowing in the brightening sun.

Glowing, not shining. And green, Casey noticed. A sickly, toxic green that had no place in the animal kingdom. Belonged to no creature he knew of, bovine or otherwise.

Like that smell. That brightly bloody coat.

"Get!" he yelled, suddenly nervous. "Go 'way! Leave me—"

"Boy!" Mr. Perkins hollered, tromping around the corner of his big, red barn. "Why in *tarnation* are ya shoutin' at my bull?"

"I didn't—I wasn't—"

"Don't make this worse by lyin' to me." Mr. Perkins lumbered over, looking none-too-pleased. Denim-covered legs *whisk-whisk-whisking* as he quick-timed it toward the gate.

An old man, Mr. Perkins—older than Nana and Pop-Pop, even—and every bit the farmer. Dirty overalls covered his round potato of a body, manure stained pitchfork clasped in one hand. A shaggy fringe of dingy grey hair surrounded his wrinkled bald pate like a halo, and when he opened his mouth, the most down-home accent came out.

Full of hard *R*s, dropped *T*s, those long, long *A*s people around here were fond of. That odd word 'ayuh' most people used, which sometimes, but not always, meant 'yes'.

"I heard ya hollerin' clear across the pasture," Mr. Perkins complained, lumbering to a halt. "Can't talk to cattle that way, boy. Scares 'em. 'Specially this one." He slapped the bull on the flank, earning himself a sharp *moo* of complaint. "This here's a sensitive stud, not some ruttin', nasty beefer. If ya want 'im to do somethin', ya gotta talk pretty to 'im. Isn't that right, big guy?"

He tickled at the bull's lip, chucking it under the chin.

The bull *lowed* loudly, backing away. Nipped a pesky fly from the air and ground it between its teeth.

*Gross.*

"See? Told ya. Refined bovine. That's what he is." Mr. Perkins smiled, exposing a whole mouthful of square-off horse teeth, pulled a filthy rag from his pocket and mopped at his sweating brow. "*Phewy,* but it is a *hot* one!"

"Yes, sir. Very, sir," Casey murmured, staring fixedly at that bull. "What—What *kind* of bovine, exactly?"

"What?" Mr. Perkins blinked, honestly perplexed.

"The bull," Casey said, leveling a finger. "What kind?"

"Why, the best stud bull money can buy!" Mr. Perkins tucked his thumbs under his overall straps, preening proudly. "Guy at the stockyard called it a Bimini Angus. That's *European*," he said, tipping a wink.

Casey frowned doubtfully. His knowledge of livestock might be dodgy, but thanks to Sister Anna and her knuckle-cracking yardstick, his geography was on point.

Bimini was *not* in Europe. He was like ninety-nine percent sure of that. Tried to tell Mr. Perkins as much, but the farmer just *tut-tutted* and waved him away.

"Got no time for yer jabber-jawing and bull oglin', son. Yer granpappy sent ya over here to help me with my fences, right?"

"Uh...yeah..." Casey scanned the line of fence post stretching in either direction, most of them decidedly leaning, barbed wire lengths sagging in between.

"Good! Now climb over that gate and get to helpin'."

"Uhh..." Casey pointed to the bull sidling up behind Mr. Perkins.

"Don't ya worry 'bout 'im, boy. Bimini here's a sweetheart, ain't ya, handsome?" He whacked the bull's shoulder, *hee-hawing* like a donkey.

A snort of annoyance, and the Bimini Angus—which Casey's ten-year-old mind immediately shorted to Bimiangus, Bimini Angus being a mouthful to pronounce—lowered its head, backing a step away.

It, not he. Technically, bulls were male, and 'he' the appropriate pronoun, but the Bimiangus was such a monster, Casey just couldn't think of it that way.

Despite, you know, the enormous wang.

The bull stomped a cloven hoof, giving the farmer a good glare. Bellowing, "*Moo-moo-moo-haroo!*" at the top of its bovine lungs.

Casey cringed, backing away from the gate. "What's it doing?"

"Aw, don't be a-feared, boy. Bimini here's just bein' friendly." Mr. Perkins *hee-hawed* a second time, swatting the bull on the rump, laughing harder when it nipped at his hand. "Now hop on over here and help an old man out."

"Umm..." Casey pointed at the bull again, standing right in front of the gate.

"Don't mind 'im." Mr. Perkins shoved at the bull, grunting when the bovine shoved right back. "Now, climb on up—there ya go," he said, nodding encouragingly as Casey tentatively mounted the fence. "Give 'im a little nudge with yer foot and he'll move right outta the way."

Casey shook his head quickly—Nana warned him about touching strange bulls—scooting along the top of the gate before dropping down, landing as far away from the bull as possible.

The Bimiangus *lowed*, soundly surprisingly disappointed. Turned when they did, heavy hooves tearing at the pasture's thick carpet of green-green grass, and *clip-clop-clomped* behind them as Casey and Mr. Perkins headed across the pasture to the big, red barn at its center.

# Two

"YA EVER STRUNG barbed wire, boy?" Mr. Perkins asked, conducting an impromptu interview as they walked.

"No, sir."

"Dug fence posts?"

"Nope."

"Mixed cement?"

"Uh-uh."

"Ya ever done *any* kinda work related to fences or fence materials?"

"Helped Pop-Pop paint that stretch over there last year." Casey pointed to the line of board fencing running closest to Nana and Pop-Pop's house.

"Huh." Mr. Perkins frowned, thick fingers scratching at the wrinkled, sunburnt crown of his head. "Not really applicable to what I got planned, but yer all I got, so I 'spose ya'll have to do. Back off there Bimini," he growled, swatting at the bull bumping up against his butt.

The Bimiangus snorted, barging between them, crowding Mr. Perkins out of the way so it could snuffle at Casey. Covering him in sticky, stinking snot.

*Gross. Gross-gross-gross-gross-gross.*

"Told ya he's a friendly bull." Mr. Perkins smiled widely, flashing those big old horse teeth. Stopped in front of the barn and trundled the front doors open. "Likes ya, son. Just wants some attention."

"Yeah. Yeah, I see that." Casey tucked up his arms, skirting around the Bimiangus and its flailing tongue as he slipped into the barn.

Not to be outdone, the bull primly followed him in. Clomped around and generally made a nuisance of itself—kind of like an overeager puppy, having to stick its nose into everything it found—the smell of it even stronger in the barn's enclosed space.

Casey kept one eye on it, and the other on Mr. Perkins farting around. Grabbing up shovels, and rakes, and every other kind of tool imaginable and loading them into a creaking, old wheelbarrow with a distinctly flat tire.

"Here. Ya'll need these," he said, parking the wheelbarrow outside. Dug around in a pocket and passed a well-worn pair of work gloves to Casey, keeping a second set for himself. "Postholer'll do a number on those soft hands a-yers without some protection."

Casey blinked, offended. Turned his hands over, and admired the hard-earned calluses on his palms.

They weren't soft. Not anymore, anyway. Not after weeks of working around the farm.

Mr. Perkins walked away before he could argue the point, heading for a lean-to shelter attached to the side of the barn. "Back in a jiff," he called over his shoulder. "Just need to fire up the tractor and bring 'er 'round."

Casey scratched his head, wondering why they needed a tractor of all things to erect a fence.

"Roll that 'barrow over there," he continued, hairy arm lifting, pointing at a stretch of fencing running in front of Nana and Pop-Pop's house. "Bull's been leanin' on damn near everythin', that stretch more'n the others. Think maybe he's got a thing for yer grand mama's pies." Mr. Perkins brayed laughter as climbed into the tractor's rusted metal seat. Turned the key and fired it up—engine revving, spewing a dark cloud of smoke as he put the tractor in gear and backed it up.

Alone with the Bimiangus, Casey soon found himself covered in snot. Stupid bull simply would *not* leave him alone. Kept bumping into him and knocking him around, butting insistently with its drippy, sticky snout.

"Go 'way," Casey growled, dodging yet another poking. Grabbed up the wheelbarrow's handles when the bull came after him and shoved its fat tire between them to hold the bovine at bay. "Leave me alone, ya stupid thing."

The Bimiangus snorted—a rough sound of complaint. Lowered its head and budged at the 'barrow, those weirdo green eyes looking even more weirdo and green than ever. Glowing like twin, hundred-watt bulbs in its head.

"Stop it." Casey snapped, holding tight to the 'barrow as the bull tried to knock it out of the way. "You are *not* touching me, you slimy, creepy thing. Now buzz off!"

A snort and the bull tossed its head. Second snort and it slammed that same head against the side of the 'barrow, ripping it from Casey's hands.

Tools went flying, scattering in a wide fan across the grass. The 'barrow flipped over, tumbling a few times before settling on its side, leaving Casey standing there, staring in disbelief at his empty hands.

A *rattle* and *chuff* and the tractor wheezed over, stopped with a squeal of rusted metal, engine's tone changing as Mr. Perkins stuck it in neutral and leaned off the side. "What in tarnation is happenin' here, boy?"

"I—He—" Casey pointed at the bull, *lowing* innocently, snout snuffling at a spilled shovel. "I was just—"

"Messin' about, from the look-a things."

"I wasn't! I swear! The bull—"

"Pick up them tools, boy." Mr. Perkins glowered sourly, jamming the tractor into gear. "Roll 'em over to that fenceline while I dump this load." He jerked a thumb at the trailer attached to the tractor's hitch, eased the clutch out and rolled away, trailer bouncing along behind him as he puttered his tractor across the pasture.

Casey rounded on the bull, waggling a finger in its cow-eyed face. "This is *your* fault, ya know."

The look the Bimiangus gave him said differently. The cloven hoof it scraped at the ground.

Casey swallowed hard, backing away from it. Reached blindly for the wheelbarrow and righted it, stacking the dropped tools inside. Bent over to retrieve a glove torn from his hand and almost jumped out of his skin when a warm, wet nose pressed against his buttocks, leaving a slimy stain on the seat of his jeans.

So much for overeager puppy. Evidently, Mr. Perkins' bull had a little Mississippi leg hound in him.

Casey smacked at the bull's nose without thinking, and received a *whuff* of hot breath in return. Straightened and found the Bimiangus standing right behind him, green eyes blazing with bovine anger.

Or hunger. Like a dog with a steak dangled in front of its face.

"N-N-Nice bull," Casey stammered, backing away. "Good bull."

The Bimiangus *huffed* like a bellows, cloven hoof swiping at the ground. Another step backward and Casey fetched up against the 'barrow. Circled around it and grabbed the handles, pivoted and raced for the fence.

"*Moo-haroo!*" the Bimiangus called, thumping feet following after.

Casey put his head down, pushing for all he was worth. Ditched the barrow when he reached Mr. Perkins and his tractor, spilling ass over tea kettle when the bull slammed into him, stepped *over* him, and knocked into a fence post on the other side.

He hit the ground and lay there, winded, staring at the blue-on-blue sky overhead. Squinted, shading his eyes as Mr. Perkins' potato shape loomed over him—fists on his hips, wrinkled face twisted up in a decidedly disapproving sneer. "Ain't no way to treat a 'barrow, boy."

Never mind that he'd just been freight-trained by a bull.

"Yes, sir. Sorry, sir," Casey answered, dusting his hands as he picked himself up.

"Water," the farmer ordered, pointing. "Run back to the barn and get a hose so we can mix up some cement."

Casey turned his head, staring across the long, long stretch of grass behind him. Snuck a look at the bull—barreled headlong into a fencepost, seemed to have knocked itself silly—and took off before it recovered.

"Make sure ya turn the water on before ya hoof it all the way back here!"

Casey raised a thumb to show he'd heard, not wanting to slow down enough to look back. Ran a lap around the barn when he reached it, located the water spigot and turned it on.

*All* the way on. Full blast, because Mr. Perkins hadn't specified how *much* water he needed and there was just no *way* he was retracing his steps just because the old man couldn't give good directions.

A quick hunt to find the hose Mr. Perkins wanted—coiled up by the barn doors, trailing length leading to the spigot—and Casey gathered the lot of it up, hanging it over his shoulder.

Turned around and ran smack dab into the Bimiangus sneaking up behind him with that dribbling, snot-encrusted nose of its already deployed.

Knocked his *own* self down this time, grousing when he landed on his rump. Fumbled for the flowing end of the hose around and shoved it in the bull's face, landing a shot right between its green-Mother-Nature-never-intended eyes.

Pissed that bull off something terrible—better believe that. Not necessarily the best idea, in hindsight, but it did make the Bimiangus back up a bit. Just enough for Casey to dive away, carrying the coiled-up hose with him, *whip-whip-whipping* over his shoulder, giving him a serious case of rug burn as it unwound and paid out.

Back to the fenceline, then, with the Bimiangus predictably following after, hoofed feet pot-holing the ground. Casey chugged along ahead of it—sides heaving like a bellows, fast-diminishing coil of hose growing heavier by the minute. Stumbled to a halt when he reached Mr. Perkins, side-skipping a *second* train-wrecking from the

Bimiangus—thing really built up a head of steam, did *not* know how to slow down—and bent over, sucking hard at the air.

"Hose," he huffed, pointing. "Water," he added, flailing a hand at the barn.

Mr. Perkins looked at him, and at the coiled-up hose lying by his feet. The wet-faced bull licking water from its end. "Why's my bull all wet?"

"Thirsty," Casey gasped, shrugging, earning himself a suspicious look.

"Empty that barrow," the farmer ordered. "Not like *that*," he amended when Casey tipped it on its side, dumping the tools all over the ground.

"Sorry," Casey muttered. Straightening as the Bimiangus *bump-bump-bumped* against his butt.

"Ya know, ya say that a lot, but ya don't look like ya mean it."

"Sorry," Casey repeated, not knowing what else to say.

Mr. Perkins squinted suspiciously, like he thought Casey might be giving him lip. "Right. How's about we get workin'. See that fence?" He pulled Casey close, wrapping an arm around his shoulders, drowning him an old man stink that was one-part Aqua Velva and two-parts stale sweat. "See how it's leanin' outward?"

Casey nodded, holding his breath.

"Need to shore it up a bit or the whole thing'll come down. So what we're gonna do is—ya listenin' to me, boy?"

"Yes, sir," Casey answered, stumbling a step as the bull pressed against his side. "Trying, sir."

"*Shoo*, bull." Mr. Perkins reached around, swatting at the Bimiangus' withers.

The bull snapped at him, teeth just missing the farmer's fingers. Green eyes fairly rolling now. Glowing like two blazing suns.

And hungry again. Angry-hungry, like before.

"Well, now. Ain't we sassy." Mr. Perkins huffed out his *hee-hawing* donkey laugh, swiping at the bull's head.

"Wouldn't do that," Casey said faintly. "He doesn't like that," he warned, backing a step away.

"What? *This*?" Mr. Perkins slapped the bull's flank, smiling like a loon. "That there's two thousand pounds of grade 'A' bull, son. Little thing like—*yow-ow-ow!*" he cried, clapping both hands to his butt. "*Ya bit me!*" he screamed, rounding on the bull, eyes wide with disbelief. "What was that for?"

The Bimiangus groaned, bass voice rumbling in its throat. Licked at its blood-speckled lips, scooping bits of denim into its mouth. A plug of fat and meat torn from Mr. Perkins buttock.

"Told you. I told you," Casey breathed, heart racing, thumping like kettle drums in his ears. "He doesn't like that. He really doesn't like that."

Mr. Perkins nodded sickly, sliding a step away.

The bull stalked after him—*stalked,* not shambled. One cloven hoof stepping sedately in front of another, dainty as a show horse being put through its paces.

And all the while, those green eyes glowing. Spinning and swirling inside its monstrously-wide face.

"What—What're ya doin'?" Mr. Perkins whispered, mouth hanging open, sucking hard at the air. One hand clutched at his damaged buttocks, blood leaking between his fingers, pattering in droplets that stained the grass. "I was *nice* to ya!" he shouted—angry, terrified, slowly backing away. "Why'd ya have to go and bite my bum like that, Bimini?"

"*Moo!*" the bull bellowed, long neck stretching, spinning eyes flaring with poison fire. "*Moo-haroo!*" it insisted, shoving at the farmer, pushing him up against the fence.

A *whuff* and its lips skinned backward, displaying squared-off, yellow teeth. Sharp-edged fangs that gnashed and chattered, keeping time with its mincing steps.

"Hell with this," Mr. Perkins decided, staring down the barrel of that bovine gun. A glance at Casey and he shrugged his shoulders, clipped off a brief, "Yer on yer own, boy," and high-tailed it. Abandoning Casey there in the pasture as he kicked up his heels and ran away.

Well, waddled, Mr. Perkins being old and potato-shaped—a bit long in the tooth and fat around the middle for actual running. Scampered right quick, though. Holding tight to his shredded, bleeding rump the entire time. Didn't *stop* scampering until he reached the far side of the pasture and monkey-climbed over the fence near his house.

"He left me," Casey whispered, staring after the farmer in disbelief. "He really left me."

Adults weren't supposed to do that. They weren't supposed to *abandon* kids to scary monsters and insane livestock, they were supposed to *protect* them from them.

"*Moo*," the Bimiangus agreed, reading his mind. "*Moo-haroo*," it chortled hungrily, hoofed feet churning the grass into mud.

"No," Casey whispered as the bull clopped near. "Run," his mind urged him, but his legs went all noodly. Threatening to drop him right there.

Another step closer, the Bimiangus' chest muscles rippling, neck stretching, lips writhing around those bloodstained teeth. Bits of Mr. Perkins' jeans and buttocks stuck between them like pieces of spinach. Only bloody, and pink. Dirty and blue.

A flicker of its tongue and the stench of an abattoir washed over him, filling Casey's nose with a hellish corpse stink. A moan and the bull lipped at him, tasting his flesh. Thinking to eat him like Mr. Perkins. Gobble him right down.

Casey about-faced and ran for it, stumbling on uncertain legs. Didn't stop to look, didn't even stop to *think*, just sprinted for the fenceline and squeezed his body between two rows of barbed wire. Ignoring the sharp points that snagged his clothing, scraping at the skin beneath. Squiggled through, pants leg catching, panicking for a minute before pulling himself free. A sob of relief and he scurried across the grass strip separating Mr. Perkins property from his grandparents' board fence. Breath hitching and catching as he clambered up one side, jumped down and sprinted flat-out for Nana and Pop-Pop's house.

# THREE

"SAFE," CASEY GASPED as the kitchen door banged closed. Leaned against it with his legs trembling beneath him, lungs working so hard he thought he might throw up.

"Casey?" Nana stepped away from the counter, rolling-pin in hand. Bits of flour and pie crust clinging to her gingham-checked apron as she turned toward the door. "What on earth has gotten into you?" she demanded. "And why is your face all blotchy?"

Casey scrubbed at his face, smearing the dirt, and sweat, and tears clinging to his cheeks. Trapped sobs, hiccupping inside him. Heart beating like a rabbit hopped up on Pixie Stix. "Mr. Perkins," he said, cringing as the Bimiangus bellowed behind him, calling out in its yodeling voice.

"What about Mr. Perkins?" Nana asked, brows drawing downward. "Casey. Have ya been actin' up again? Did Mr. Perkins send you back here—"

"No!"

"Casey..." Nana lifted her rolling pin, slapping it against her palm. "Willfulness and shenanigans are the devil's dastardly duo, mister, and I will *not* have either in my house."

"Dastardly duo?" Casey's shoulders twitched, hitching with giggles entirely inappropriate to his current situation.

"What's so dang-blasted funny?" Nana asked, frowning now. Looking annoyed.

"Dast—D-Da-Dast—" Casey choked, hands pressed to his mouth to hold the laughter inside.

A blast from Foghorn Bullhorn killed it instantly. Turned the laughter into a scream trying to claw its way up Casey's throat.

"Are you quite done?" Nana asked him.

Casey nodded, *huffing* and *puffing* behind his hands.

"Good. Now get back outside to that pasture before—"

"Huh-uh," Casey told her, shaking his head.

The bull was out there. No *way* he was going back outside.

Nana's frown deepened, rolling pin beating a rhythm as she smacked it against her hand. "Your Pop-Pop promised Mr. Perkins—"

"Left me. Don't *care* what he promised."

"Left you? Who left you?"

"Mr. *Perkins.* That bull got angry and—"

The kitchen door flew open. "Casey! What're ya doin' in here?" Pop-Pop demanded, stepping into the house.

"Mr. Perkins ran away and—"

"Thought you said he left you," Nana cut in.

"I—He—I—"

"You best not be fibbin' again, young man."

"I'm *not*! He *did*! He ran away and left me all alone!"

"Now why would Jim Perkins do a thing like that?" Pop-Pop asked, folding his arms.

"Because the bull bit 'im."

"Bit 'im," Pop-Pop repeated. "Why would that prized bull of his—a bull he dotes on like some mother hen—go and bite 'im?"

"'Cause it's *evil*." Casey invested the word with all the earnestness a ten-year-old could muster, pointing a finger at that self-same evil thing as the Bimiangus let loose with another bugling call. "See? *Ya see?*" He waggled a finger at the bull outside. "It's out there, Pop-Pop. It tried to *eat* me—"

"Eat you?" Pop-Pop's woolly-bear eyebrows lifted, tickling at the buzz-cut edge of his hairline. "Evil *and* a man-eater." He whistled appreciatively. "That is *some* combo."

"Clem." Nana's rolling pin stopped moving, resting now in her cupped palm. She nodded over Pop-Pop's shoulder, stepping in behind him as he turned around. "It *is* out there."

"Damned thing's *always* out there, Evie. Screwin' up the fences somethin' terrible. Look at it." He gestured at the fenceline, shaking his head in disgust. "Look how bad that stretch is leanin' now."

Nana *did* look. Pushed the screen door wide open and took a good, long look around. "Don't see Jim out there," she noted.

Pop-Pop frowned, stepping outside himself. "Tractor's there. Tools, wheelbarrow, everythin' else."

But no sign of Mr. Perkins. Not anywhere in that pasture.

"Maybe you should go check on him," Nana suggested.

"Yeah. Yeah, I just might." Pop-Pop glanced over his shoulder, turning that frown of his on Casey. "Get his side of the story while I'm at it."

"I'm not fibbin'," Casey insisted. "That bull is evil. And creepy. And it bit Mr. Perkins right here." He turned around, pointing a finger at his keester. "Right on his butt."

"Maybe." Pop-Pop eyed him doubtfully, gaze drifting to the Bimiangus *mooing* its fool head off, prowling up and down the barbed wire line. "Stay here," he said, waving at Casey, sharing a worried look with Nana as he stepped out the door.

\*\*\*

Pop-Pop returned at sunset—head down, hands stuffed in his pockets, the sky blood-red behind him as he stopped just outside the kitchen, taking a good, long look at the Bimiangus prowling the fenceline. Nudging at fenceposts with its nose.

Scanned the sky as thunder rumbled in the distance—a surly, muttering sound. "Storm's comin'," he said, grimacing as he stepped inside.

"Sounds like," Nana murmured, face worried. Eyes flicking to Casey watching the both of them from the kitchen table. "Everything all right, Clem?"

Pop-Pop shook his head—not a 'no' shake, an 'I don't know' shake, Casey knew the difference—lumbering across the kitchen to give Nana a peck on the cheek. Smiled at her, touched a finger to her iron-grey hair, smoothing an errant curl behind her ear.

That smile betrayed his own worry. Pop-Pop didn't smile much— he used to, supposedly, but lost his smile with part of a foot while off fighting in some long-forgotten war—and the smile he showed Nana now didn't quite look right. Didn't *feel* right, somehow.

Smiles were meant to be happy, but Pop-Pop's almost looked sad.

"Run up and take yer bath, Casey." Pop-Pop stroked Nana's cheek not even looking Casey's way. "Yer grandmother and I need to talk for a bit."

Casey didn't like the sound of that. "But—"

"Go," Pop-Pop told him—weary, not angry. "Please," he added, looking Casey's way.

Casey blinked. That 'please' really threw him. Made him nod without realizing he was doing it, feet turning of their own volition as he slipped his chair, hurry across the kitchen with its dark-oak cabinets and sunshine-yellow linoleum. Across the attached living room—more dark oak on the floors and walls, floral patterns on the overstuffed sofa, the two matching chairs—and up a creaking set of stairs.

Slowed halfway to the second floor of the old farmhouse, creeping soft-footed the rest of the way. Sat down in the shadows at the top to eavesdrop on his grandparents' conversation.

"Well? Did you find Jim?" Nana asked, voice drifting from the kitchen.

"Ayuh."

"And?"

"Got bit all right," Pop-Pop told her. A sharp *pop!* echoed through the open doorway, followed by the *glug* and *fizz* of beer flowing into a glass.

Casey's eyes widened, surprised by that unexpected sound.

Pop-Pop rarely drank anything stronger than water or Nana's lemonade. Things must be dire for him to hit the hard stuff before dinner.

"Big, nasty thing," Pop-Pop continued. "Right on his bum, just like Casey said."

"Told you," Casey muttered. "Told you I wasn't fibbin'."

"Oozy, red thing. Worried it was infected, so I drove him over to the clinic for some shots and bandages. That's what took me so long. Doc gave him some painkillers and antibiotics. Really knocked Jim on his ass. He's sleepin' it off at home now."

"You sure he's all right on his own, Clem? Maybe—"

"I'll check in on him in the mornin'," Pop-Pop assured her.

Silence after that. Silence for a long, long time.

"So, what happened?" Nana asked a few minutes later.

"Hmmm?" Pop-Pop sounded distracted.

"Why'd the bull bite him?"

"Well, 'cording to Jim, our grandson's to blame."

"Me?" Casey was indignant. "What did I do?"

"Said he was messin' with that bull all mornin'. Yellin' at it, pushin' it around. Supposedly sprayed it with a hose at one point. Lord only knows why."

All true statements, but the context was missing. Casey stared at the light spilling from the kitchen, tempted to march right down there and set the record straight.

"Casey said that bull was evil. *Creepy.* Really seems to bother him."

"Not sure about evil, but Jim did say that bull was pesterin' Casey a bit." Pop-Pop was quiet a moment, grunted and chuckled softly. "Mentioned somethin' about it not rogerin' his bossies. Started sayin' a lotta things once those drugs hit his system."

"Oh yeah? Like what?"

"Claimed he was gonna sue the government for false representation. Had this bunch-a papers he kept wavin' around, goin' on and on about how they were sellin' off surplus stock as grade 'A' beef cattle."

"Government?" Nana's tone changed, taking on a sharp note. "Is that where that bull came from?"

"Lord only knows. Never did get a good look at those papers." Pop-Pop went quiet again. "Would explain a lotta things, though. Government does like to experiment on things."

"Bet it's not a bull at all," Casey muttered. "Just some frog or somethin' that *mutated* into a bull."

"Casey," Pop-Pop murmured, so softly Casey himself almost didn't hear. "Casey and that bull."

"What?" Nana asked him.

"Just thinkin' 'bout that fence. How the piece that butts up against ours seems to've taken the brunt-a that bull's love."

"Maybe Casey's right. Maybe there's more to this than just some randy bovine protectin' its pasture."

Pop-Pop snorted. "Don't tell me *you* think it's evil."

"No. But I think it's a bull. And bulls can be mean. Especially to little boys." Nana went quiet herself. "He's scared of that bull, Clem. Really, truly scared. I could see it in his eyes."

"Little boys grow up to be big boys," Pop-Pop reminded her. "Which means little boys need to learn to stop bein' afraid-a livestock at some point."

"Oh, Clem." Nana's sigh gusted all the way up the stairs. "I need to finish makin' dinner, so why don't you go upstairs and take a long, hot soak 'til it's ready? Maybe you can finally get some-a that grease off your hands."

"Yes, Dear," Pop-Pop answered in his long-suffering voice.

Casey skedaddled in a hurry, the sound of Pop-Pop's footsteps chasing him into his room.

\*\*\*

Dinner that night was a quiet affair, with none of the chit-chat and banter Nana and Pop-Pop usually shared. Pop-Pop ate in silence, looking only at his plate while Nana chewed her food, watching him, mostly. Glancing at Casey now and then.

Quiet, the three of them. Everything in that house. Quiet, and quiet, and quiet, except for the bull honking ceaselessly outside.

"Is Mr. Perkins gonna be all right?" Casey asked at one point, heaping macaroni salad onto his plate. Nana put mustard in it as well as mayonnaise, an addition that made it extra good. "The medicine the doctor gave him—it'll fix up that bite, right?"

Silence from both ends of the table, Nana and Pop-Pop both looking his way

"What?"

"How long were ya listenin'?" Pop-Pop asked him.

"I don't know." Casey shrugged uncomfortably, stabbing a pork chop with his knife.

"All right then. Let's try it this way." Pop-Pop set his fork and knife down and folded his hands in front of him, elbows resting on the table. "How much did ya hear, Casey?"

Casey fiddled with his fork, wondering if he could get away with a lie. Remembered the bar of soap upstairs with his name on it, and decided it wasn't worth it the risk. "Most of it," he admitted, pushing food around his plate.

"Huh," Pop-Pop grunted, and that was it. No lecture, no explosion, just, "Huh", and Pop-Pop picked up his knife and fork, cutting his pork chop into bites he methodically fed into his mouth.

"You're—You're not mad?"

"Nope." Pop-Pop chewed and swallowed, spearing another bite. "Wanna tell me yer side of it?"

"Well..." Casey fidgeted, suddenly self-conscious. "It—It kept bumping into me," he started. "And—And following me around. *Everywhere*, Pop-Pop. And it kept *licking* me, and knocking up against me the entire time I was in Mr. Perkins' pasture." He snuck a look at Pop-Pop, trying to gauge his face. Glanced at Nana sitting across from him, seated at the opposite end of the table, and decided to go all in. "It—It chased me," he admitted, staring at his plate.

"Chased you?!" Nana's eyes widened "Clem—"

"He's a stud bull," Pop-Pop reminded her. "Stud bulls are ornery. Chase everythin' around when their blood's up."

"Ornery's one thing. Chasin', attackin', that's another."

"Oh, come now, Evie—"

"No," she said firmly. "I know you promised Jim he'd help him, but I won't send Casey back there. Not if that bull's turned mean."

"Don't worry." Pop-Pop lifted his glass, taking a drink. "He's not goin' back."

Casey heaved a sigh of relief.

"Jim don't want him back."

Ouch, that hurt.

"Says he's a troublemaker and he don't want him over there stirrin' up his livestock."

Ouch again. Total rejection. Casey slumped in his seat, wishing he could just slide under the table and disappear.

He finished his meal in silence, consumed two pieces of pie in silence—Nana slipped him the second when Pop-Pop wasn't looking—watched an hour and a half of TV in silence. Made the weekly phone call to his parents—couldn't really do that last bit in silence, but he didn't talk much—and afterwards went straight to bed.

*Early.* To avoid the silence between Nana and Pop-Pop. And, honestly, because he was dead-dog tired. Felt like he could sleep, and sleep, and sleep some more.

Unfortunately, the Bimiangus had other ideas. Casey just *happened* to look out the window as he pulled back the covers and spotted two eyes staring back at him from the darkness. Bright green and glowing, hovering by the fenceline.

Two eyes and a darkly shaped body—wicked, and crooked, and hardly bovine at all.

"*Moo! Moo-harooo!*" the Bimiangus called, moaning into the pale moonlight.

"Go 'way. Just go 'way," Casey willed it, pulling the covers over his head.

"*Mooooo! Moo-moooo-haroooo!*" the Bimiangus insisted, ululating into the night.

"Shut up-shut up-shut up," Casey whimpered, sticking his fingers in his ears. Grabbed a pillow and stuffed it over his head for measure as the Bimiangus called up to his window, yodeling through the long hours of the night.

# FOUR

"YOU LOOK TERRIBLE," Nana said, when Casey came down for breakfast the next morning.

"Couldn't sleep," he said, yawning. Drowning the pancakes Nana set in front of him in a small sea of butter and syrup. "Stupid bull kept me up all night."

"Clem..."

Pop-Pop rattled his paper. "He learned to sleep with traffic outside his window. He'll learn to sleep through a noisy bull."

Easy for him to say. Pop-Pop and Nana were both hard of hearing. And they both took their hearing aids out at night. Nothing short of an explosion would wake Casey's grandparents from their beauty sleep.

"Clem." Nana waited until Pop-Pop lowered the paper. "You're goin' over there anyway. Why dontcha ask Jim to put the bull in the barn at night?"

"C'mon now, Evie."

"Just ask," she urged him.

"Fine. I'll ask him." Pop-Pop folded his paper, setting it down. "But I can't guarantee he'll do it."

"No one's asking you to, dear." Nana smiled sweetly, tipping a wink Casey's way.

"Five minutes," Pop-Pop warned, tapping a finger to his watch. Pulled a list of chores—what he called 'fix-its'—from the front pocket of his bib overalls. The one right on his chest.

Casey shoveled food into his mouth, alternating bites of pancake with nips of bacon.

"Four," Pop-Pop said, prompting Casey to eat faster. Guzzle his orange juice and slam the glass down. "Time," he called, shoving back his chair, heading for the door.

Casey dumped his dirty dishes in the sink and hurried after, stepping outside into a swamp-humid morning—blood-red sun rising on the horizon, blood-red bull beneath it, standing predictably at the fence.

Watching. Waiting. Gazing at Casey with those toxic, creeptastic green eyes.

"Rain would be nice," Pop-Pop said, wind ruffling his shirt as he scanned the cloud-strewn sky. "Ain't had any in almost three weeks now. Crops need it. Might cool things off a bit, too."

"Yeah. Maybe," Casey said, distracted by the Bimiangus' gawking. Eyes drifting to the herd of cows behind it, clustered on the far side of Mr. Perkins' pasture.

Keeping as far from that bull as possible, or so it seemed to Casey. Like the herd didn't want anything to do with it. Didn't want to be anywhere *near* the Bimiangus.

"Whatcha lookin' at?" Pop-Pop asked as they walked along. Booted feet crunching across the dirt and gravel driveway as they headed for Nana and Pop-Pop's barn. No cows in there—Nana and Pop-Pop sold those years ago—but they kept a few chickens. A squad of loudly honking geese. "Whaddaya see over there?"

"Cows."

"Cows, huh? How exotic." Pop-Pop glanced over his shoulder, smile twitching his lips. Stopped and frowned, eyes flicking across Mr. Perkins' field, the roughly two-dozen cows in residence. "Huh. Used to be more of 'em. Don't remember Jim sellin' any off..." He trailed off, scratching at his head. Turned around and took a second census of the field. "'Spose maybe some of 'em are still in the barn." He chewed on that a moment, looking from the barn in question to Mr. Perkins' ramshackle farmhouse parked behind it and to one side. "Ah, well. I'm sure they're around here somewhere. C'mon, Casey. Maybe they're just hidin' on the other side of the barn."

Pop-Pop set off down the driveway, making for the poorly-maintained county road at the end.

"Wait!" Casey called, catching up with him. Slipping around his grandfather when the bull followed after them, flicking its slimy, pink tongue. Putting Pop-Pop's body between himself and the Bimiangus for protection in case that fence over there finally came down. "Where are we going?"

"Jim's house." Pop-Pop pointed across the pasture to the dilapidated old house sitting about five-hundred yards behind the red cow barn. "Barn needs paintin', but it's hardly the weather for it. Don't quite trust ya on yer own with any of the *other* chores on my list," he patted the wrinkled piece of paper in his bib overall's pocket, "and if I leave ya with yer Nana, she'll just spoil ya with cookies. Figure the best thing for everybody is if ya come with me."

Everybody meaning Pop-Pop, not Casey. The best thing for Casey was to go back to his bedroom and play with his toys.

"*Moo,*" the Bimangus rumbled, as if reading his mind.

Casey grabbed Pop-Pop's arm and hugged it to him, clinging protectively to his much larger and far more bull-savvy grandfather as they rounded the corner at the end of the driveway, following the chipped and broken asphalt of the county road to Mr. Perkins driveway, just a quarter of a mile down.

A driveway remarkably similar to Nana and Pop-Pop's—rutted and weedy, fence on one side, grass on the other—except for the house at the end.

Pop-Pop maintained his house—an 1800s vintage Federal with bright-white clapboard siding and dark-green trim—fixing problems as they appeared so things didn't get out of hand. Mr. Perkins obviously didn't subscribe to that strategy. Didn't seem to care about fixing much anything at all.

From the looks of things, the Perkins house actually used to be something pretty special—a quaint, two-story Victorian with gingerbread molding around the windows, sprinkled liberally around the edges of a spreading front porch. But somewhere along the way— likely when the current Mr. Perkins took up residence—things obviously went south. Porch front sagging, gingerbread turning to rot, the entire thing ramshackle and decaying—even the paint seemed to have given up the ghost.

Casey approached that building with trepidation, holding tight to Pop-Pop's hand. Mounted the creaking, decomposing steps and stood behind him as Pop-Pop rapped his knuckles against the glass-fronted door. A second knock when no one answer, and Pop-Pop pushed the door open, shouting, "Jim?" as he stepped inside.

"Who is it?" a grousing voice yelled back. "Whaddaya want?"

"Probably best if ya stay here," Pop-Pop decided, parking Casey by the front door. "Won't be long," he said, nodding as he mounted a set of stairs, heading for the second floor.

Casey huddled up in a corner, arms wrapping around his middle.

Inside was as bad as outside, except darker—curtains closed, no lights on anywhere—and dustier. Everything covered in a fine layer of grey powder, motes of it swirling in the heat-thick air.

Close feeling to that front room, the others to either side. Furniture filled every nook and cranny. Knick-knacks and chachkies decorated every shelf, and tabletop, and otherwise available surface. Hot as blazes with the windows all closed. Fans turned off, leaving everything stuffy and stopped up.

Casey hugged himself tight, eyes flicking around the junk-packed house. Not daring to touch anything because pretty much everything in here looked both antique and highly breakable. Not even *wanting* to sit down on anything because of the piss and dank stink of the place, Mr. Perkins' Aqua Velva and sweat-reek an undercurrent drifting down the stairs.

He gazed up them, willing Pop-Pop to hurry. Grateful for being left out of a no doubt unpleasant encounter—he could hear the bickering already, Pop-Pop's bass rumble punctuated and often overridden by Mr. Perkins' more nasally, querulous voice—but wanting out of here. Wanting out of this house, off this property, safely ensconced in Nana's kitchen with its bologna sandwiches and swiveling army of fans.

Fifteen minutes he huddled down there—an eternity in ten-year-old time—before a door banged above him and Pop-Pop appeared, *thumping* heavy-footed back down the stairs. "Miserable, pig-headed old cuss," he muttered, sweeping past Casey without a word.

He stomped into the kitchen and rifled through drawers, snagged a curl-covered and much abused phone book from beneath a *Crockpot Treasures* cookbook and flipped it open, searching for a number scrawled sloppily on the inside cover.

"Pop-Pop?"

"Hang on, Casey. Just need to call the doc."

Doctors meant sickness. Casey clapped his hands to his face, covering his nose and mouth, eying all the potential sources of contagion in that cluttered-up, junked-up house.

Pop-Pop, meanwhile, was swapping information with someone on the phone—back facing Casey, making it hard to hear much of anything, though the words 'bite' and 'infection' came through clearly enough.

"Can ya just come over?" he asked, twisting to check on Casey, handset pressed to his ear. "An hour. Great. Thanks, Doc. I'll be here." Pop-Pop hung up, sucked in a breath and wandered back to the front hall. "Looks like we've got some time to kill." He glanced at the stairs, considered and rejected any idea of going back up in the space of about two seconds. "Let's go check on them cows," he suggested, herding Casey toward the door.

"Check on the cows? As in, go in the *pasture* and check on cows!" Casey balked on the front porch, spotting the Bimiangus waiting, having followed them all the way around to Mr. Perkins' house. "Think it's followin' me, Pop-Pop," he whispered, hiding behind his grandfather's thick shape.

"Nonsense, boy. He's probably just curious. Jim don't get many visitors these days." He pried Casey loose and held him at arm's length. "Now I know yer scared-a that bull, but ya just stick close to me and everything'll be just fine."

Casey wasn't so certain, but when Pop-Pop strode away, he left him with two choices: run away like a scaredy-baby back to Nana, or man up and stick with his grandfather.

Or head back into Mr. Perkins' house, an option that never even occurred to him until he was already at the fence.

"*Moo*," the Bimiangus greeted him, stomping a hoof, pressing against the fence.

"Umm... Pop-Pop? I'm not sure—"

"Stick with me, Casey." Pop-Pop grabbed his arm, dragging Casey over as he flipped the latch in a people-sized gate. "I'll keep ya safe."

He stepped through, bold as you please, towing Casey along behind him. Dropped his shoulder and hockey-checked the bull when it crowded close, knocking it off-balance, sending it stumbling, *harooing* away.

"Go, Casey. Go-go-go!" Pop-Pop slung him around, propelling him toward the nearby barn. Let go and raised his arms, yelling, "Hooooo! Beefer-beefer-beefer! Hooooo! Ya big stud!" as he waved them over his head.

Casey stared a moment, distracted by his grandfather's distraction. Caught a flash of one of glowing, green eye turning toward him and took off, sprinting for the barn's back door.

Slammed into it with the *thump* of cloven hoofs chasing behind him, fumbled the latch, muttering, "C'mon-c'mon-c'mon," until he finally got it. Yanked the door open and slipped inside.

A *clunk* and *rattle* as the bull slammed into the wall behind him, shaking the barn's back wall. Pop-Pop hollered, *shooing* it away, maneuvering around the bull to approach the door himself.

Casey backed away, fumbling in the semi-dark for a light switch, located it with his fingers and cut the overheads on.

Blood. Blood everywhere. Soaking the dirt floor, painting the walls. He stepped on something squishy, glanced down and saw it was an eyeball. Kicked it away and watched it bounce across the floor, skipping and spinning before fetch up against a leg.

A leg attached to a body—*Bovine*, his mind registered, *Cow*—sliced neatly open, guts spilling grotesquely as it lay there on its side.

More bodies around it—rent and torn, bloody and broken and definitely, most certainly dead.

Casey opened his mouth, scream climbing up his throat. Turned around and ran straight into Pop-Pop just stepping through the door.

"Whoa-whoa-whoa! What's—?" Pop-Pop broke off, eyes widening. "Sweet Mother Mary." He hugged Casey's shaking body to him, taking the horror show in. "Close yer eyes, Casey," he whispered, voice hushed in that place of death. "Hold onto me," he said, lifting Casey, wrapping his arms around him as he wove a path through the cow corpses, heading for the doors on the far side.

Leaving the Bimiangus behind them, snorting angrily, kicking impotently at the back wall. Sneaking quiet as a ninja through the front door to set Casey on his feet outside, holding tight to his hand as he escorted him back home.

"Inside," Pop-Pop ordered, lifting Casey over the barbed-wire fence. "Tell yer Nana I'll be back soon as I can."

"*Moo-haroo!*" the bull bugled behind them, feet *thumping* as it trotted around the barn. "*Moo-haroo!*" it protested as Casey crossed the grass divider and clambered over the board fence.

Looked back when he reached the far side, worried about leaving Pop-Pop alone with that ass-biting monster. Guilty for *wanting* to leave him and get far, far away from that bloodstained barn.

"Go. Get," Pop-Pop ordered, walking along the fenceline, circling wide as he backtracked to the barn.

The Bimiangus watched him—angry, accusing, shifting like he meant to charge. Grumbled and slouched over, *lowing* and moaning as it knocked at a leaning post, renewing its assault on the fencing near Nana and Pop-Pop's house.

Casey backed away from it, one slow step at a time. Wiped at his face when the first raindrops hit it, glancing skyward as the heavens opened up.

His foot slipped, skidding on slick grass blades, dropping Casey onto his backside. He scrambled back up in an instant with the raindrops pelting his head. Soaking his jeans, sticking his t-shirt to his back. Spun around and raced for the side door leading into the kitchen, ripped it open and ducked inside.

"You're back early. Again." Nana frowned, looking past him to the door. The yard and pasture outside. "Where's your grandfather?"

"I-I-I—He-He-He—" Casey turned and pointed back the way he'd come.

"He checkin' on Jim?"

Casey nodded, shivering. "Doctor. Back soon." The shivers got worse, making him tremble and twitch.

"Upstairs," Nana ordered. "Out of those wet clothes. I'm makin' a roast for dinner, so you can help me pinch these green beans when you're done."

Casey nodded wordlessly, walked stiffly across the kitchen, through the living room and up the stairs. Stripped off his clothes and lay down on his bed, watching the rain pour down outside and the wind whip it around. Listening to the mutter of approaching thunder as the trembling eased, there in his overheated room.

Closed his eyes and saw red-red-red—guts, and feet, and the Bimiangus' glowing green eyes. Twitched and jerked upright, shoving off the bed, digging through the dresser's drawers for clean clothes.

"Casey?"

"Coming, Nana!"

He tugged his jeans on, slipping a fresh t-shirt over his head. Slouched down the stairs to the kitchen and plunked down at the table across from Nana, vaguely aware of her watching him worriedly, as he dipped a hand into the bean bowl between them and started snapping and pinching in silence. Eyelid fluttering every time the Bimiangus' complaints drifted through the kitchen's screen door.

"TV says it's gonna be a real rager." Nana nodded to the storm outside. "Wind's pickin' up already. Figure once it blows in, it'll be two, maybe three days before it moves on."

Which sounded just fine to Casey. Rain meant fewer chores outside. Less chance of running into that bull.

He twitched again, eyelid fluttering like butterfly wings as the Bimiangus yodeled and groaned.

"You wanna tell me what happened over there?"

Casey grabbed another bean, shaking his head.

Nana pursed her lips, snapping off a stem. "All right. Maybe later."

That look again—part curiosity, part concern, all of it directed at him.

Casey ignored it—he really, really didn't want to get into things right now—and concentrated on pinching beans, working his way methodically through the bowl.

Nana left him alone after that, content to finish prepping the beans in silence. Shuck their way through a bowl of pea pods after, and a half dozen ears of corn.

Shared lemonade and bologna sandwiches at lunchtime, with the Bimiangus keeping them company. Singing its siren song from the fence. And afterward—with all the kitchen chores completed, nothing to do but sit there at the table and swing his feet, boots scuffing at the sunshine-yellow linoleum—Casey found time to worry. Wondering where Pop-Pop was. Why he hadn't come back yet.

"Nana—?"

The door ripped open, Pop-Pop appearing from nowhere—soaked to the bone and a little out of breath. Ducked inside and whipped off his hat, slapping it against his knee to shake the worst of the wet off.

Casey stared at him—infinitely, overwhelmingly relieved.

"How's Jim?" Nana asked, nodding to Casey, shaking her head.

"Not well." Pop-Pop eyes flickered over him. "Found 'im lyin' in bed, sweatin' like it was a hundred and twenty degrees. Looked pale as milk, Evie. Shakin' like he had a palsy." Nana handed him a towel that he swiped at his face, wiping raindrops from his arms, and neck and chest. "Took care of some chores for 'im while I was over there."

"What kinda chores?" Casey asked faintly.

Pop-Pop grimaced. "The kind I don't like."

"Oh." Casey ducked his head, staring at his hands.

"Doctor come over." Pop-Pop scrubbed the towel through his hair, draping it across the back of a chair when he was passably dry. "Said he had some kinda infection. Gave 'im a shot and some pills, but I don't think they're helpin'. If anythin' he looked worse when I went back to check on him after..." Pop-Pop trailed off, lips pressing in a hard line. "Anyway. I got some food in 'im. Some beef stock and a couple-a sandwiches I made with those minute steaks he likes."

"Minute steaks aren't proper food, Clem."

"Wouldn't eat nothin' else. 'Sides, not much else in the house, him bein' a bachelor and all."

"I could fix him a plate. Bring it over later."

"I wouldn't. Man's in a *foul* mood."

Nana was quiet a moment, lips pressed together. "Think we should take him to the hospital?"

"Should. Damn fool won't go, though. Threatened to get 'is twelve gauge if I didn't leave 'im alone."

"That's not like him." Nana sounded worried.

"Nope." Pop-Pop hesitated, considering Casey sitting quietly at the table. "How's about ya go upstairs and play for a while. Yer Nana and I need to discuss a few things."

*Adult* things, his look said. Ten-year olds not wanted.

Casey thought about objecting—ten was almost teenaged, and teenaged just about adult—but it had been a long day already, with many scary things. The last thing he needed was Pop-Pop pissed at him before being lippy and not doing what he was told.

He slipped from his chair in silence, retreating to his upstairs bedroom. Flipped open the toy box shoved under the window and stared lackadaisically at the mis-matched, hodge-podge of toys inside.

Leftovers from his own father's childhood years. Most of them far too baby-ish for his tastes, though the plastic dinosaurs were fun. And the army men. Some of the farm animals.

He snatched up a handful of all three, carrying them with him as he walked to the steps. Sat down and played with them while he snooped on his grandparents again.

"Somethin' else I wanted to tell ya, Evie."

"About Casey? Came back upset about somethin'. Jim didn't yell at him, did he?"

"No. It's not that." Pop-Pop sighed heavily, going quiet for a few seconds. "Some of Jim's cows went missin' from the herd this mornin'."

"And?"

"Dead," he said grimly. "Found 'em dead in the barn, Evie. *Worse* than dead. *Torn up.* Mutilated. Bellies ripped open, guts torn out. Blood..." Pop-Pop sucked in a breath and blew it back out. "Blood everywhere. Terrible, terrible sight."

"Casey wasn't with ya, was he?" Nana sounded breathless— shocked and upset.

"Ayuh. Saw everythin', unfortunately."

"Oh, Clem."

"Yeah. Poor little feller. No kid should see that."

Quiet again, neither of Casey's grandparent's talking. Casey himself sitting frozen at the top of the stares, mind flashing on red, and guts, and wide-wide eyeballs as he gripped a dinosaur tight.

"You tell Jim?" Nana asked, voice hushed.

"No. He's got enough to worry 'bout. Don't need to know about somethin' gettin' in the barn and tearin' up those cows right now."

Another space of silence, longer than the last.

"So, what'd you do with 'em? The cows, I mean."

"Buried 'em. Dug a hole with the backhoe, stuck 'em inside and covered 'em up. Funny thing? Cows won't go anywhere near the place where those dead 'uns are buried. Stay all the way on the far side of the pasture. Far away as they can get." Pop-Pop grunted, work boots *thumping* heavily as he kicked them off. "Bull don't seem fazed a bit. Still not interested in those bossies, which is odd—should be all over them females, 'specially with it rainin' and such. Just stands by that fence all day, though. Doin' his darndest to knock it down. Annoyin' cuss," he grunted. "Not sure 'bout 'evil', but there surely does seem to be somethin' wrong with it. Casey's right about that."

Things got quiet after that. Really, *really* quiet. The kind of quiet that meant adults were thinking deep thoughts.

Casey slipped away from the doorway, deciding he'd heard enough. Knocked around his room for a while, holding gladiator matches between the two dinosaurs and a couple of plastic horses until Nana called him down for dinner.

# FIVE

MORE RAIN THE next morning—oceans of it filling the sky, drenching the ground, transforming Mr. Perkins' pasture into a quagmire of grass and mud.

Wind whipping everything, blowing the raindrops sideways, pelting the side of Nana and Pop-Pops neat house.

Weather guy got it right, for once. Storm really was a rager.

Casey woke to the sound of thunder, a surprisingly pleasant change from the Bimiangus' endless serenade—a horrible, deep-throated lullaby the bull sang to him most of the night. Stumbled downstairs blinking away bad dreams and cobwebs and found Pop-Pop standing at the kitchen door, scanning the field outside.

Frowning as he did it, obviously not liking what he saw.

"What's going on?" he asked, pattering soft-footed to his grandfather's side.

Pop-Pop shook his head, frowning harder. "Herd," he grunted, nodding to the field outside.

Casey looked himself—*really* look—and realized more cows were missing. The herd less than half the size it was the day before. The cows themselves huddled up together, *lowing* mournfully in the rain. Not eating, which was decidedly uncowlike. Especially considering how *much* cows liked to chew on wet grass.

"Pop-Pop?" Casey tugged at his grandfather's sleeve. "Where are all the cows?"

Pop-Pop lowered his chin, shaking his head again.

"What's wrong with them?" he asked, breath quickening, heart pitter-pattering in his chest. "Where are they going? *What's happening to all the cows?*"

Pop-Pop's hand landed on his shoulder, squeezing hard. "Wish I knew, Casey." He flicked his eyes across the field, frowning darkly at a lump near the corner of the barn. A second blocking its doorway. Three others scattered around the pasture nearby.

"They're dead, aren't they?" Casey asked in a hushed, scared voice.

Pop-Pop's mouth opened, eyebrows twitching and wriggling in that way that said he was going to lie. Likely to spare Casey's feelings. Make him feel better about all this cow disappearance business.

Well, Casey didn't want a lie—not this time, not even to spare his feelings. Strange things were happening around Mr. Perkins' farm, and this time he wanted the truth.

"I heard you last night," he blurted, bringing Pop-Pop's wriggling eyebrows to an abrupt halt. "I know what happened to those other cows."

Pop-Pop grunted, sharing a look with Nana behind him. "Got ourselves a spy, Evie." He tried to smile, but his lips couldn't quite manage it.

Nana, for her part, just sipped her cup of coffee, staring worriedly at the door.

"It's the bull, isn't it?" Casey said, drawing Pop-Pop's eyes back to him. "Mr. Perkins' Bimiangus, it's—it's ... *doing* things to them, isn't it?"

'Doing things' wasn't very specific, but 'murder' didn't quite sound right. He honestly wasn't sure if a bull *could* commit murder, or if bovine-on-bovine violence was called something else altogether.

"*Moo-der!*" the Bimiangus called, making Casey jump. "*Moo-haroo-der!*" it bellowed, long tongue licking at its lips, lapping crimson droplets from its muzzle.

Blood from those poor, dead cows. Reams of it, coating its face, splattered across its chest.

Casey bent over and retched on Pop-Pop's boots—didn't mean to, felt kind of bad about it, but once the stomach spasms started, he couldn't make them stop.

The chicken from the night before came up first—mostly digested, a whitish-pink goo that popped out in chunks—followed by the peas and carrots—also mostly digested—potatoes and pie, a couple of cookies he filched before retreating upstairs. All of it, every last morsel and dollop of Nana's evening dinner barfed unceremoniously onto the linoleum of her kitchen, soiling the floor of this, her personal domain.

"Sorry," he managed, in between heaves. "I'm so sorry, Nana," he gasped, chucking up a last, masticated cookie.

Pop-Pop's arm wrapped around him—warm and comforting, still strong despite all his years—leading him over to the table. Turning Casey over to Nana, who sat him down in a chair. Grabbed a bottle from the refrigerator and set it down by his hand.

Casey blinked dully, staring at it.

Soda, at six in the morning. Ginger ale, because that's what you gave little boys with upset stomachs, no matter what time of day it was.

"Ya keep 'im here today, Evie," he heard Pop-Pop say. "Ya keep 'im inside and away from... *that*." Pop-Pop's lip lifted, hand gesturing in disgust. Sweeping across the Bimiangus. The pasture with its tiny, terrified herd of cows. He snagged his hat off a peg by the door, and a slicker from a coat closet off the living room, smashing the one on his head while he tugged the other on. "Might be gone a while. Need to check on Jim. After that..." Pop-Pop paused, eyes drifting to the door, the pasture, the dark lumps scattered around.

"You take care of 'em," Nana said softly, gnarled hand resting lightly on Casey's shoulder. "You see to those poor bossies lyin' outside."

Pop-Pop nodded—a single, sharp movement of his head. Yanked hard on the slicker and pushed the door open, stepping outside.

"Clem!" Nana called after him, stepping to the door. "Be careful, you hear?"

Pop-Pop nodded again—slowly this time, looking thoughtful as he did. Pinched the brim of his hat and turned away, striding off into the rain.

Nana stood by the door for a while, staring after him. Shuddering each time the Bimiangus let loose with an agonized *moo*. Retreated to the kitchen table a few minutes later and finished her coffee. Poured herself a second cup, pulling a box of graham crackers down from the cupboard while she was at it, that she set in front of Casey.

Popped the top on the bottle of soda and poured half of it into a glass. "You drink that, Casey. It'll make your stomach feel better."

Casey's clenched up gut didn't want much of *anything* right now, but he sipped at the ginger ale to make her happy. Nibbled at a graham cracker when she pressed one on him, chasing each microscopic mouthful with the tiniest thimble of soda.

For an hour, they stayed that way—Nana sipping coffee at one end of the table while Casey nursed his ginger ale at the other. And then, Nana sat up straight, eyes widening as she caught sight of something behind Casey, on the other side of the kitchen door.

"What is it?" Casey whimpered, not daring to look. Convinced it was the Bimiangus busting through the fence, marching right up to that door.

"Fire," Nana told him, wrinkled face pale. "There's a fire over yonder."

And not just *any* fire. A bonfire. A *huge* conflagration blazing in Mr. Perkins' pasture, a safe distance from his red, red barn. Smoke billowing in a greasy, grey cloud, heat turning the rain to mist around it as the wind swirled, whipping at the flames.

A gust blew through the screen door—Nana hadn't closed the storm door on the other side, preferring the cool breeze and a little wet on her linoleum to a stuffy, stopped up house—flooding the kitchen with a blood and char stink. A smell of meat cooking that set Casey's stomach to churning, ginger ale and graham crackers percolating in his gut.

Cows inside that bonfire. A mound of dead flesh slowly being consumed by flame. The deep-throated growl of an engine rumbling through the air as a backhoe trundled from behind Mr. Perkins' barn.

"Pop-Pop," Casey whispered, reaching for Nana's hand.

She curled her fingers around his, holding tight to his hand. Eyes locked on the door—that window on Mr. Perkins' pasture—as Pop-Pop angled for the bonfire, bucket lifted, the rounded blob of some many-legged shape perched stiffly inside.

Stopped short in front of the flaming cow pile, backhoe's wheels locking, heavy machine skidding sideways in the mud. Tipped the bucket forward and dumped another cow carcass on top of the mound of burning others, flames leaping and twisting as they sucked in more fuel.

"Why's he doing that?" Casey whispered. "Why didn't he just bury them like the others?"

"There's too many, honey. Ten cows at least in that pile. Take an age to bury that many, even with the 'hoe to help out."

Nana stood, holding tight to Casey's hand. Stepped around the table, moving closer to the door.

Worry in her eyes, reflecting the fire's light back. A look of concern that creased her wrinkled brow, pressed her thin lips in a hard line.

"There's something wrong with those cows, isn't there?" Casey asked her in a soft, hushed voice. "Something so bad Pop-Pop's burning them to cover it up."

"You go upstairs, Casey." Nana never even looked at him, just patted him on the shoulder, releasing his hand. "You go play in your room a while. I'll come get you when it's time for lunch."

Casey opened his mouth to object, but Nana just flicked her fingers, *shooing* him away. "Yes, ma'am," he said meekly, collecting the box of graham crackers.

Took the half-full bottle of soda with him—no sense wasting good ginger ale—as he snuck out of the kitchen and retreated to the safety of his room.

# SIX

NANA BROUGHT A bowl of soup up to Casey's room for lunch—chicken noodle, another icky-tummy favorite. Swapped a plate of salted crackers for the cinnamon sweet grahams, leaving Casey with a kiss and a fond pat on the head.

And another ginger ale, much to his surprise. Unprecedented, Nana allowing him two sodas in one day. Of course, he didn't see her for the rest of the afternoon. Didn't hear a peep out of her either, which worried him after a while. And when he crept from his room to check on her, sneaking down the creaking, wooden stairs, he found Nana standing in front of the kitchen door—one arm wrapped around her middle, the other tugging the end of her iron-grey braid.

"Nana?"

"Fine, Casey. Everything's fine," she told him, never once looking his way.

Casey tip-toed back to his room, figuring that was the best place for him right now. Half-heartedly played with his toys until Pop-Pop returned that evening, kitchen door banging as his booted feet *thumped* inside.

"Terrible thing, Evie."

That's how Pop-Pop started. No 'Hello', no 'What's for dinner?', no preamble at all. Just *thump, bang,* and straight to the bad news—that was his grandfather's way.

Casey crept to the top of the stairs and listened, too scared to go down.

"Poor cows," Pop-Pop said, sighing. "Those poor, poor cows."

"Torn up?" Nana asked quietly. "Like the others?"

"Worse," he told her. "It was worse this time."

"How?" she asked, just as softly. As if afraid to talk too loudly.

"Can't really explain it. Half of 'em..." Pop-Pop sighed again. "Half of 'em weren't even in one piece by the time I found 'em, Evie. One of 'em..." He trailed off, going quiet a moment. "One of 'em had its skin missin'."

"Oh, Clem."

"Terrible, Evie. Most terrible thing I've ever seen. Like some rabid animal had been at 'em. Blood everywhere, body parts everywhere. Live ones—the ones that *weren't* kilt—just standin' there, shiverin'. Scared outta their minds. Feel sorry for 'em, Evie. I really do."

"What did you do with them, Clem? Those other cows, I mean. What did you do with the ones that are left?"

"What *could* I do? Jim sold them other hundred acres. All he's got left is the house, the barn, and that one fifty-acre field. Tried to get Jim to call his cousin, have the cows trucked over to *his* farm, but he wouldn't have it."

"So you left them there? With that horrible Bimini Angus bull?"

"Had to," Pop-Pop told her. "Shut 'em up in the barn to at least get 'em outta the rain. Bull shouldn't be able to bother 'em in there, so they should be safe until I can figure somethin' better out."

Couldn't keep cows shut up in a barn forever—even Casey knew that.

"And Jim?" Nana said softly. "How's he doin'?"

"Worse and worse. Looks like death warmed over. Still won't let me take 'im to the hospital."

"Maybe I'll try," Nana offered. "If Iris were still here—god rest her soul—she'd make Jim go. Now that she's passed on... well, I guess that leaves me to be the voice of reason."

"I don't know, Evie. I'm not sure he'll listen."

"Worth a try."

Pop-Pop grunted, so Casey supposed Nana won that round.

Things went quiet after that. *Stayed* quiet all through dinner— Nana and Pop-Pop not talking, Casey fresh out of ideas for things *to* talk about. An hour of TV after dinner—same old shows, some program set in an office that was probably funny but made no sense to Casey at all—and he slipped upstairs, knocked his toys around for a while before putting them away, and himself to bed.

Snuck a look at the windows—he just couldn't help himself—and saw green eyes staring back at him, the Bimiangus standing its lonely guard in its usual place.

Quiet, like everything else this evening, which Casey found odd. Pressing against the fence, gazing forlornly at his bedroom, but not *mooing.* Not calling out.

Had to wonder about that. What was going on in that creepy creature's creepy mind.

He flipped over, putting his back to it, listening to the rain patter against the glass as the wind whistled around the old house's corners.

The *creak-creak-thud-thud* of Nana and Pop-Pop mounting the stairs to their own bedroom, floorboards popping and cracking beneath their feet.

"G'night, Casey-bear," Nana whispered, poking her grey head in.

"'Night, Nana," Casey mumbled, snuggling down, enjoying the silence while it lasted. Slipped to sleep, and started to dream.

Strangely, he knew it was a dream, from the very first moment.

The windows gave it away. Open windows, not shut up tight to keep the rain out. No storm outside, either, just the Bimiangus moaning at the moon.

He ignored it at first, focused only on his toys. Gripping a T-Rex in one hand, and a stegosaurus in the other, growling *"Rowr!"* as he smashed the two together, letting them battle for supremacy—a power struggle involving much grunting and gnashing of teeth.

All supplied by Casey, of course. The dinosaurs were just toys, even in this dream.

In a surprising twist of fate, the stegosaurus got the better of the T-Rex—dodging its stubby, front legs to take a nip at its gut—and seemed on the verge of taking it down. But a bellow from the bull outside and Casey froze, dinosaurs forgotten.

Something about that call didn't sound right. Well, to be honest, *nothing* about the bull's intonations sounded right, but this *particular* one sound more wrong than usual. An almost *fevered* note to its call. A heavy *thud* that came with it, followed by an awful, wet splattering. Like someone throwing paint against a wall. A fan of puddle water spraying across a bus stop as a truck drove by.

Couldn't imagine anyone was painting out there at this hour. And no buses out there. Not even the yellow Twinkies that picked the farm kids up when school was in session.

"I'm dreaming," Casey reminded himself. "Dreams aren't supposed to make sense."

He pinched himself—*hard*—to see if he'd wake up. Slapped his cheeks when that didn't work and only succeeded in hurting himself more.

Apparently, waking up from dreams wasn't quite as easy as the movies made it out to be.

Casey sat there on the floor, gripping his dinosaurs tightly, listening to the splattering sounds outside rise and full. The groans of the Bimiangus increasing in volume before suddenly, unexpectedly cutting out.

Stared suspiciously at the window, waiting for it all to start right back up again. Shrugging when it didn't. Going back to playing with his toys.

Changed his mind about the stegosaurus winning, and let the T-Rex stomp all over it.

It was cooler, after all. And had bigger teeth—a gaping, snaggly-toothed maw.

He snarled, showing his own teeth as the T-Rex snuck in, tearing at the stegosaurus' pointy-plated back. Chomped, and growled, and chewed its way toward the stego's neck, the final death blow sadly interrupted by a flare of light outside.

Bright and blinding, bathing Casey's bedroom in a red-orange glow.

Curious, he ditched the dinosaurs, climbed on top of the toy box and pressed his nose to the bedroom window's glass.

Blinked in disbelief at a world engulfed in fire. Flames licking across the walls of Mr. Perkins' barn, dancing gleefully as they consumed the roof. Screaming, as the cows inside roasted—trapped by the very same doors meant to secure them from the Bimiangus.

A second fire behind that barn—Mr. Perkins' moldy old Victorian farmhouse blazing merrily—and in between, a vast ocean of flickering, yellow-red flame. The pasture itself erupting, eating its way to the fence.

And outside Casey's window—the only thing that *wasn't* actually on fire—was the Bimiangus, *moo-harooing* as its jaws stretched wide, spewing out blood.

"No," Casey breathed. "I'm dreaming. This isn't real."

He flinched, covering his ears as more screams split the darkness—human, this time. Angry and in pain.

A man's screams, keeping time with the Bimiangus' bellows. Wanting *out* of that blazing field, and into the green, green yard on the other side. The quaint little house where Casey sheltered, watching the world burn from his window upstairs.

"No," Casey whimpered. "Go 'way. Leave me 'lone."

"*Moo! Moo-moo-haroo!*" the Bimiangus screamed, driving Casey away from the window, back to the floor.

He scooped up the dinosaurs, holding them protectively in his hands. Hard, plastic edges digging into his palms, piercing the skin to let his blood well out. "Go '*way*," he repeated, rocking back and forth. "Leave me '*lone*," he told the dream, and this time it actually worked.

The nightmare shattered, leaving Casey staring wide-eyed at the ceiling, sucking in deep, shuddering breaths. He rolled out of bed, stumbling for the window, searching for the house and the barn, the ever-diminishing herd of cows.

Found the one and the other—neither on fire, both looking just fine—and the Bimiangus outside his window, standing where it always did. Green eyes glowing sickly in the darkness, yellow-red flames crawling across its crimson-hided skin.

On *fire,* despite the rain pouring down around it. *Lowing* loudly as it pressed against the barbed wire fence. It spotted Casey in the window and called out to him, bovine voice hungry, needing, not the least bit in pain.

"This can't be real," Casey whispered, staring in horror. "I must still be dreaming."

The Bimiangus *mooed* a negative, tossing its massively oversized head. Shoved hard at the fence, hell bent on knocking the entire thing over. Barbed wire stretching to the point of breaking as the fence posts leaned, and leaned, and leaned some more.

"No. No-no-no-no-no," he said, head whipping side to side. Watching in horror as the flames reached the bull's withers, flowed across its back. Snaked along the long line of its neck, and washed over its face, skin crackling and popping, flames dancing on the tips of its horns.

And all the while, the Bimiangus seemingly oblivious. Unaware it was slowly burning to death.

"Stop, drop and roll, buddy," Casey giggled, panicked, hysterical laughter wrenching at his gut.

He choked it down on the edge of lunacy. Worried if he let it out, he'd never recover. Really, truly flip out and go completely, nut-bags insane.

The wind shifted, driving rain against the window. Wafted dark smoke and the stench of charred meat and burning blood his way. The Bimiangus shifted too, cloven hoofs tearing at the swampy pasture, hide peeling, hanging in tattered shreds that dangled between its thick legs.

Horrified, Casey scrambled away from the window, tripping over his own feet as he backed across the room. Squeaked in fear when he fetched up against the wall on the other side, sliding along it until he reached a corner where hunkered down—legs tucked up to his chest with his arms wrapped around them, keening as he rocked back and forth.

Couldn't see the bull from that corner, but the flickering light of the flames consuming its body showed clearly through the window's glass. Worse, he could still *hear* it—its voice, its hooves, the crackling skin pulling away from its body.

He covered his ears, trying to block it. Dropped his eyes and stared at the floor boards, telling himself this couldn't be happening. That nothing—not even the Bimiangus—could survive being set on fire.

Five minutes he sat there, hugging his legs tight. Five long, drawn-out minutes of the Bimiangus screaming, while Casey waited for it to die.

Lay down on his side and curled up in a ball when that noise went on and on. Wanting it all to stop. The bull to give it over—dead, gone or disappeared, he really wasn't picky, he just wanted it to leave him alone.

An hour passed, then two, each minute marked by the slow ticking of the smiley-faced cow on his bedside clock. Casey blanked at some point—dozed off, or zoned out, or simply lost it—and when he came back to himself, the light outside was gone, and the Bimiangus had mercifully gone quiet.

Confused, suspicious, Casey lay there a while longer, curled up tight on the floor. Unfolded from his cramped, protective position and climbed to his feet, tip-toing to the window, peering fearfully through the glass.

The flames had gone out, but the Bimiangus stood right where he'd left it—a dark shape, looking even darker now with the fire gone, and the night's shadows gathering 'round. Not much light out there, with the sky occluded, clouds blanketing the stars, but the moon peaked through briefly—just a crack, just for a few seconds, long enough for Casey to get clear look at the bull below him, crispified hide hanging in shreds.

Long enough to see it was chewing on something. Square teeth grinding as its jaws moved side-to-side.

Casey flashed on Mr. Perkins, and the bloody hole the Bimiangus had nipped in his butt. On the dead cows lying inside the barn. The blood and intestines staining the floor.

"*Moo?*" the bull queried, stomping a sharp hoof. "*Moo-haroo?*" asking him to come down and play. Come outside and give him a smooch.

Casey grabbed the shade, rolled in a tight curl at the top of the window, dragged it closed and threw himself toward his bed.

Burrowed under the twisted, sweat-soaked covers, hiding beneath them while the Bimiangus screamed for him to come outside.

"Nana," he whispered. "Pop-Pop. Help."

They had to hear this—no *way* anyone could sleep through all that bloodcurdling chatter—and yet, despites his prayers and pleading, despite the fact he peeked from under the covers and *stared* at their door, Nana and Pop-Pop never came to save him. Couldn't *hear* him *or* the Bimiangus—not with their hearing aids removed for the night.

Alone in his room, Casey lay wide awake, staring at the floor, the ceiling, the walls. And across the hall, his grandparents kept sleeping. Blissfully oblivious to the horror outside their house.

# Seven

THE BULL QUIETED by morning, bellows giving way to the barrel-chest *lowing* normal cattle used to greet the dawn.

Casey hid under the covers anyway, too afraid to come out. Listened to the creak of the floorboards as Nana stepped into the hall and padded downstairs to fix breakfast, Pop-Pop's heavier tread following soon after, stair risers protesting as he descended to the first floor.

With his grandparents awake, the house didn't seem quite so scary. The world outside his covers safe enough for him to poke his head out and take a look. Abandon the bed and dress in his work clothes when Nana hollered up the stairs, letting him know breakfast was ready.

Didn't look at the windows, though. Couldn't quite make himself do that. Knew good and well the Bimiangus was out there waiting for him, but he wasn't quite ready to deal with that just yet.

A check of his fly—Nana always seemed to notice when he left the barn door open—and he stepped into the hallway and descended the stairs. Slowed when he reached the kitchen, the damp smell of rain-drenched smoke stronger here, almost choking as it mixed with the smell of Nana's bacon.

"What?" Nana asked, brows knitting, following the line of his sight to the kitchen door.

"Didn't you hear it?" he asked, edging across the room. "Can't you *smell* that?"

"Not sure what yer..." Pop-Pop twisted, staring. "Sweet mother of Jesus," he swore, chair scraping across the linoleum as he shoved it back and stood.

"Moo," the Bimiangus greeted him as he walked over to the door. Looking decidedly worse in the watery sunlight—fur missing, skin missing, tendrils of smoke rising from bloody, raw meat.

Strips of hide littered the ground beneath it, hanging from its belly in ragged-edged lengths. It *mooed* at the people studying it from the kitchen, dipped its head and ripped clods from the ground. Worms wriggling, desperate to get free as it slurped them into its mouth.

Grinding the grass, and dirt, and fleshy pink things to a slurry with its sharp-edged teeth, shitting half-digested lumps out its other end.

"Good Lord," Nana gasped, hand pressed to her lips.

"What the hell happened to that bull?"

Pop-Pop sounded shaken. Stared wide-eyed through the door.

"Not supposed to say hell," Casey said faintly. "Go to hell for sayin' hell, Pop-Pop."

"How is it alive?" Nana breathed. "How is it even *standin'*?"

A gust of wind blew the smell of it into the kitchen, filling the room with a burnt skin and smoldering manure stink.

"Ugh! Clem! Close the door." Nana backed away, voice high-pitched and wavering—a tone Casey had never, *ever* heard come out of her. "The police," she said, grabbing Pop-Pop's arm. "Clem. Ya gotta call the police!"

"And tell 'em what, Evie? That there's a burnt-up bull standin' in my neighbor's pasture tearin' holy hell outta the grass?"

"Well, we've gotta do *somethin'* don't we?" Nana waved at the smoldering bull. "Put the thing out of its misery at least."

"How?" Pop-Pop demanded. "Ya know I got ridda all my guns a few years back."

"Jim," Nana said, arms folding. Head tilting to one side.

"Jim? Jim ain't in no shape to be shootin' no gun."

"But he *has* guns. And I'm sure he'll let you borrow one once you show him how much that bull of his is sufferin'."

"Maybe."

"Clem. Please." The arms unfolded, Nana's hand touching gently at Pop-Pop's arm. "I know you don't like that bull—either of you," she added, turning a look Casey's way, "but no creature, no matter how vicious, deserves to live like that."

Pop-Pop was quiet a moment, thinking that over. Grimacing as a patch of seared skin sloughed off the bull's back. "Yeah. Yeah, yer right, Evie. I'll go ask Jim if I can borrow his pistol. Shot in the brain should bring that critter down."

He grabbed his boots and yanked them on, shaking his head at Casey when he scooped his up, too.

"Not this time," Pop-Pop told him, holding up a hand. "I want ya stayin' inside with yer Nana. Wanna make sure I know where ya are when that gun goes off and that bull goes down."

Casey stifled a sigh—relieved, if truth be told. "Yes, Pop-Pop," he said, faking disappointment.

Hadn't really wanted to go out there, but he felt like he should. Like it was *expected*. Didn't want anything to do with the Bimiangus, though. Hoped to never go near it again.

He dropped his boots and wandered over to the table, sat down and grabbed a piece of bacon from a plate. Nibbled it nervously while Pop-Pop tied off his boots and grabbed up his hat, stuffing it on his head.

"Ya keep him inside, Evie." A check of the chin strap, snugging it tight so the wind wouldn't whip his hat right off.

"You know I will, Clem." Nana caught his gaze and held it, hugged him tight and let him go as Pop-Pop pulled the kitchen door open and stepped into the storm outside. "Careful, Clem," she called after him, prompting Pop-Pop to look back.

A nod and he left them, pulling the door to.

"What do we do now, Nana?" Casey asked softly. Worried now. Scared just thinking about Pop-Pop being out there all alone.

"Wait, honey. We just wait a while," Nana told him.

She sat down and finished her coffee, watching the bull outside all the while. Poured a second cup but never touched it. Just picked it up and set it down—nervous gestures, Nana twitchy and distracted, which wasn't like her at all.

Gathered up all the dirty dishes when the coffee went cold and started washing them in the sink. Eyes lifting to the window now and then. Scrubbing sponge moving in circles that slowed, and hesitated, and finally stopped.

"What is it?" Casey asked, twisting to look out the window. "What's—"

"Call an ambulance!" Pop-Pop yelled, bursting wild-eyed through the door. "Tell 'em there's been an accident. Jim Perkins's been hurt."

"Jim?! What—"

"Just *do* it, Evie!"

Nana whirled, crossing the kitchen in three, quick steps. Snatched the phone's handset from the wall and dialed 9-1-1 with shaking fingers as Pop-Pop ducked outside again, slamming the door shut.

"Hurry!" Nana said, hanging the handset back up. Turned around, wringing her fingers, eyes flicking from the door to the window and back to the door again. "Casey-dear. Run outside and tell your grandfather they're comin'."

"Yes, Nana," Casey whispered.

"Asked them to send the police with the ambulance, just in case. You tell him that, too."

"Yes, Nana," Casey repeated, tugging on his boots.

"Didn't think to ask for the fire department." She chewed her lip, looking even more worried now. "I'm sure they'll call for them if they're needed, don't you?"

"Yes, Nana. I'm sure they will, Nana."

She nodded distractedly, hand lifting, tugging at the end of her braid. "Go on now, Casey." She flicked her fingers, sending him away. "You go find your Pop-Pop."

"Yes, Nana," Casey said, already out the door.

# EIGHT

THE POLICE CARS and ambulance arrived together, sirens wailing, lights flashing in sparkling red and blue colors that speckled the rain, scattering fireworks in the air. Casey flagged them down as they approached the driveway, waving them in so they knew where to go.

Soaked to the bone from the pouring rain, but hardly even noticing. Watching the police cars pull in and pass by in a little procession—six of them, every last cruiser the county had to offer.

Lone ambulance bringing up the rear, playing caboose to that train of wailing police sirens. The cops drove right past Casey, too intent on reaching the crime scene to stop and give a soaking wet kid a lift, but the ambulance driver took pity on him. Stopped and pushed the passenger door open, inviting Casey in.

Driver's nametag read 'Sloane', guy in the back had 'Winslow' stitched to his chest.

Casey nodded to them both, slipping in, pulling the door closed. "Over there," he said, nodding to the gate in the board fence, its twin on the barbed wire side. "Turn in there," he told the driver as the ambulance bumped along, bouncing and jouncing on the rough dirt track.

"Kiddin' right?" Sloane shared a look with his partner. "Been rainin' three days, kid. Ground's mush. Rig'll get stuck if we drive in there."

Casey shrugged. "That's where Mr. Perkins is at. Only other option is to squeeze all your stuff between the fence somewhere else."

Wouldn't work, and the EMTs knew it. No way they could stuff a stretcher and medical kit, not to mention two six-foot, two-hundred-pound guys, between six strings of barbed wire fencing.

"Right. Here goes nothing." Sloane turned the wheel, cringing as he rolled through both gates. Spun it again, turning in the opposite direction this time, as he rolled the ambulance into the pasture—driving fast enough to keep the rig from bogging down, but slow enough to prevent the wheels from losing traction. The back end from fishtailing and spinning them around. "Where we goin' exactly?"

"Fence line," Casey told him. "Part closest to my grandparents' house." He pointed to the house in question so the EMT wouldn't get it confused with Mr. Perkins' Victorian dump.

"Lotta fence, kid. Could ya be a bit more specific?"

"See that guy?" Casey pointed through the windshield at his grandfather standing in Mr. Perkins' pasture.

"Yeah."

"See that lump on the ground in front of him?"

"Yeah."

"That's Mr. Perkins."

"Shit. Killed out here?"

"Pretty sure." Casey kept his voice calm. He was proud of himself for managing that. "Know where you're going?"

The EMT nodded.

"Okay. Slow down a bit then." Casey checked the side mirror and—surprise-surprise—found the Bimiangus clopping wetly behind the ambulance, dogging Casey's steps even now. "Great," he muttered, pushing the door open.

"What? Wait! What're ya—"

"It's fine. Just let off the gas a bit."

Sloane frowned dubiously, slowing the ambulance to a crawl.

Casey jumped out when he judged it safe enough, ground squishing as he landed, covering his boots in water and mud. Hurried away with his boots squishing and squeaking, squeezed between the barbed wire layers and scurried across the wet grass, climbing the board slats of Nana and Pop-Pop's side of the fence.

The Bimiangus *clip-clopped* behind him, sliding to a halt on the far side. *Moo-harooed,* staring forlornly after Casey, ignoring poor, dead Mr. Perkins lying close by his feet.

"Pop-Pop!" Casey yelled, waving his arms over his head.

Pop-Pop waved back, grim-faced and soaked through. Rain dripping from the brim of his hat, running in streams like tears down his face.

He pointed at Casey, and the bull in front of him. Pivoted and stabbed a finger to one side.

"Got it!" Casey called back, flashing a thumbs up. Turned away and trotted along the fence line, drawing the Bimiangus away from Mr. Perkins's body—wouldn't do to have him attacking the EMTs, after all—stopping when the bull was far enough away.

Watched from there, as the emergency crews set to work.

Well, the ambulance crew did. The cops parked in front of Nana and Pop-Pop's house, realized they couldn't drive through from there to the location of the body, and turned around en masse, rolling their cruisers back *down* the driveway to the double gate providing access to the field.

Half of them promptly got stuck in the mud, tires spinning uselessly while the troopers cursed behind the wheel.

The rest swaggered from their vehicles, swearing at the mud and shit strewn everywhere, and ambled over to Mr. Perkins crumpled body, joining the EMTs already there.

Eight of them in that field. Eight uniformed emergency personnel—most of them armed, all of them highly-trained—standing in a circle around poor Mr. Perkins.

"He dead?" one of the cops asked.

Badge said 'Wise'. Casey almost laughed. Officer Wise wasn't very wise at all. Didn't take any training to see Mr. Perkins was dead-dead-dead.

Wise turned to the EMTs and repeated his question while the rest of his fellows milled about.

The EMTs looked at each other and shrugged. "Check 'im," Sloane told his partner, nodding at Mr. Perkins' body.

Winslow grimaced, considering the muddy muck in the pasture. Squatted down and pressed his fingers to Mr. Perkins' throat. "Yup. Dead all right."

"What happened?" Wise asked, turning Pop-Pop's way.

"Bull." Pop-Pop jerked a thumb at the Bimiangus.

"Bull? Yer kiddin'."

"Nope." Pop-Pop pointed to the piles of manure and burnt cow flesh scattered around Mr. Perkins' body. "Looks like bullshit to me. Ain't no *other* bovine types around here, least-ways."

Casey had missed that before, but pop-Pop was right. No other livestock in that pasture anywhere. Not one single cow in sight.

*Still in the barn,* he thought. *Still locked up from last night.*

Wise frowned at the farmer's dead body, noting the gas can clutched in one hand, the blowtorch lying near the other. "Mr. Perkins got a history of abusin' his livestock?" He caught Pop-Pop's eye, nodding meaningfully to the Bimiangus and its crispified hide.

"Not that I know of. Prized stud bull, that one. No cause to be hurtin' it."

Wise studied Pop-Pop a moment, turned and surveyed the pasture. "Bull was alone? No other cattle?"

"Twenty cows not so long ago," Pop-Pop told him.

"But?"

"Killed. Most of 'em anyway."

"Killed?"

"Murdered, ya might say."

"Murdered." Wise barked a laugh. "Can't say I've ever heard murder used in relation to livestock."

"Don't know what else to call it."

"Huh." Wise looked his grandfather up and down, squatted beside Mr. Perkins and took a closer look. "Turn 'im over," he ordered, waving at the EMTs.

Sloane and Winslow looked at each other, shrugged and did as he asked.

Mr. Perkins looked worse once they turned him over. Half his head was gone—eye missing, skull missing, even an *ear* missing— leaving a ragged-edged, stoved-in hole on one side.

"Murdered, ya said. By him?" Wise pointed at the Bimiangus. And when Pop-Pop nodded. "He the one killed the cows too?"

"Nope. Wolves."

Casey stared in disbelief.

Pop-Pop had outright lied. And to law enforcement, no less—he was pretty sure that was a federal offense.

"Wolves," Wise repeated, looking dubious to say the least. "Ain't no wolves 'round here that I ever heard of."

"Hear wolves're movin' back in. Takin over a lotta places they vacated before."

"Huh." Wise still didn't look convinced. He stood and backed away as the EMTs loaded Mr. Perkins' body onto a stretched and trundled it over to the ambulance.

Pop-Pop stared after it, looking surprisingly sad. "Somethin' got in that field, anyway. Tore up the cows."

Wise's eyebrows lifted.

"Laid their bellies open," Pop-Pop told him. "Scattered their entrails everywhere."

"Wolves," Wise repeated.

"That's what it looked like to me. Jim swore up and down it was that bull killed those cows, but wolves seemed more likely."

"And Mr. Perkins here went after this bull because...?"

"Told ya. Thought it was killin' his cows."

"And just why would he think that?"

"'Cause it attacked him a few days ago."

"Attacked him? Why would his prized bull attack him?"

"Who knows," Pop-Pop shrugged. "It's a bull. They ain't really known for bein' rational. Bit 'im right on the ass, though. Ya can see for yerself." Pop-Pop nodded to the EMTs lifting Mr. Perkins' body into their rig.

"Hold up," Wise called, hurrying over, grabbing Winslow by the arm. "Roll 'im over and pull his pants down."

"Huh-uh. You do it."

"Me?" Wise looked squeamish.

"We respond, we fix 'em if we can, cart 'em away if we can't. Nothin' in my job description about strippin' dead bodies for the local police's amusement."

"Fine," the cop huffed. "I'll do it myself." Wise grabbed Mr. Perkins around the middle and heaved his body over, unclipping the straps of his overalls so he could shuck them down and get a look at the bite on his hairy butt. "Well now. That's a doozy."

Sloane leaned over, checking himself. "Looks infected. You take him to the hospital?"

"Nope. Wouldn't go. Called a doctor in, got 'im some more medicine. *Tried* to take 'im to the hospital, but the ornery son-of-a-bitch wouldn't go."

"Was he feverish?"

"Oh yeah."

"Hallucinating?"

"Maybe."

"That would explain it." Sloane turned to Wise. "Guy was sick, feverish, probably whacked out of his gourd. Gets it in his head that bull's been killing his cows, comes out here and torches it. Case closed."

"*Moo*," the bull agreed, stomping its foot. Shifted, blocking Casey's view of the scene, tongue flickering as it stretched its neck across the fence.

"Move," Casey told it, sliding a step to his left.

The Bimiangus followed him, shambling sideways through the mud. *Whuffed* when a bird landed on its back and turned its head, watching it flit about and peck at its ruined skin. A quick sniff and it darted its head forward, flicking its long, long tongue. Wrapped that slimly, pink length around the poor, unsuspecting bird and sucked it into its jaws.

*Crunch*, went the Bimiangus' teeth, chomping down onto the little birdie. Grinding it to pulp, blood and feathers falling from its lips as the bull swallowed the cheeping chirper down.

Casey grimaced, sliding another step away.

"Killed by a bull after torching it with gasoline," Wise said, drawing Casey's eyes back to the field. "That really what ya expect me to write in my report?"

"If the shoe fits," Sloane shrugged.

"Sure wish it didn't." Wise sighed and pulled Mr. Perkins' pants back up before waving the EMTs away. Watched the rig slow-roll across the pasture, and onto the muddy, dirt-track driveway, turn right and head for the road at the end. "Sick bastard, that's for sure." Wise grunted, turning around as the ambulance disappeared, heading for the county morgue. "Ya ask me, the damned fool got what he deserved. Got no call to be wanderin' around in the middle of the night, settin' his herd on fire."

"Jim Perkins was a good man," Pop-Pop said firmly. "Not sure what possessed him to do what he did, but I won't have ya talkin' 'bout him that way, Officer. Won't have ya speakin' ill of the dead."

"Good man, eh?" Wise squinted, giving him a narrow look. "Good man don't treat cattle like that."

Pop-Pop glanced at the bull, grimacing as more skin sloughed away. "Maybe," he said, nodding reluctantly. "Can ya put it down? Was gonna do it myself. but I ain't got no guns. Sold 'em all off last year. Thought to ask Jim for one, but..." Pop-Pop shrugged, gesturing in the direction the ambulance went.

"Can't," Wise told him.

"Why not?"

"County ordinance. Owner can put a sick animal down. Animal control can put a sick animal down. But you, me, yer grandson there— it's thirty days in jail and a $5,000 fine if we put that beastie down."

"Yer kiddin'."

"Nope."

"Stupidest thing I ever heard."

"Yup." Wise stuffed his thumbs through his gun belt, rocking back on his heels. "Can thank the new administration for that. Kinder, gentler bunch-a government weenies. Gonna show us hicks how we should be treatin' our animals."

"Couldn't ya just—"

"Nope. And you can't either. That bull shows up dead, I'll know it was you. Administrators'll send me back here with an arrest warrant with yer name on it."

"Goddamn animal cruelty."

"Yes, it is. But ain't nothin' we can do 'bout it."

"Fine. Can ya call animal control then? Get them down here?"

"Yeah. Sure." Wise reached to his shoulder, keying the mic on his radio as he walked a few steps away.

Pop-Pop stared after him, watching the cop as he talked back and forth with someone on the other end. Getting pretty upset at one point—hands waving, voice turning strident—and when he walked back to join the others, Casey understood why.

"Animal control's been notified. They'll be here Saturday."

"Saturday?! But it's Thursday! Ya expect me to stand by and watch that animal suffer for *two whole days*?"

"Sucks, I know. But Harvey—he's the only vet tech they got who's licensed to deal with livestock—well, Harvey's clear across the county dealing with a herd-a neglected horses or some such. Said they'd send him over soon as he's done, but Saturday was the earliest ya could expect him."

"Earliest," Pop-Pop said, glancing over at the bull, catching Casey's eye. "So it could be longer?"

"Could," Wise nodded. "Look, we gotta scour the crime scene, pick up evidence, take some photos, that kinda thing. So if ya wouldn't mind...?" Wise gestured to the house, making it clear he wanted Pop-Pop to go.

"Right. G'day, Officers." Pop-Pop nodded to each of the policemen in turn. "Don't forget to close the gate when yer done."

Wise nodded and waved, clearly half-listening, not really caring about Pop-Pop and his gates.

Pop-Pop frowned, turning away, walked across the pasture and closed both gates himself, giving the cops a sour look as he walked by. Muttering something about 'two-bit constabulary' as he collected Casey and herded him inside the house.

"What about the bull?" Casey asked as Pop-Pop led him away.

"They've got guns. It turns mean, they'll shoot it. Take care of our problem for us."

"And if it doesn't?"

"Ya heard the man, Casey. We kill it, they arrest us. Feel bad for that bull, but I'm not goin' to jail. And I'm not payin' $5,000 so I can shoot it in the head. Animal control'll be by in a couple-a days. They'll take care of it. 'Til then we wait."

Couple of days—that didn't sound so bad. Just a couple of days and it would all be over. The Bimiangus out of Casey's life once and for all.

# NINE

THE POLICEMEN STUCK around a few hours longer, collecting evidence in the pouring rain. Piled into their cruisers with their blood samples, and dirt samples, and pieces of Mr. Perkins' skull and slipped and slid across the pasture, tearing the muddy ground up. Roared down the driveway, with their red and blues flashing and their sirens screaming fit to wake the dead. Leaving the gates open behind them— never mind Pop-Pop's specific directions to the contrary.

"Damnable lazy-ass policemen." Pop-Pop grabbed his hat, stuffing it on his head. "Sheriff Bromley would-a never let his department get in such a state. Back in a jiff, Evie. Just need to shut them gates."

He slogged back out into the wind and rain, locking the gates up tight. Checked on the cows in the barn—what few were left, anyway, Mr. Perkins' herd reduced to just ten scared little bovines, now, huddled up inside that barn—and the Bimiangus in the field before heading back home.

"Why do you think he did it?" Nana asked him, broaching the subject of Mr. Perkins and the burnt up Bimiangus over dinner that night.

Casey listened quietly, eyes flicking from Nana at one end of the table to Pop-Pop at the other, fork shoveling bites of pot roast into his mouth.

"Suspect the EMT was right. Think Jim was likely off his head with fever and went and did somethin' stupid."

Nana's lips twisted, making it clear she wasn't so certain. "You really think that's all there was to it?"

Pop-Pop shrugged, jaws chewing while he sawed a slice of beef. "Not sure what else it could be."

Nana was quiet a moment, fork tines tapping against her plate. "Still think it's the bull that killed him?"

"Makes sense, don't it? Thing probably lashed out while it was burnin', caught poor Jim in the head."

"So you don't think it *meant* to kill him."

Pop-Pop shrugged, popping a bite of beef into his mouth.

"So what do we do about it?" Nana asked. "Bull's mean, and that's certain. But *Saturday*?" Nana shook her head. "Long time for an animal to suffer, mean or otherwise."

Pop-Pop grunted, chewing. "I'll take one-a Jim's guns to it in the mornin'. County and its fool ordinances be damned."

Nana nodded.

Casey wasn't quite sure if she was agreeing with the shooting, or the damning, or both.

"What about Jim's farm? Wife's dead and he's got no kids. No family at all that I know of. No one to take it over and keep things up."

"Got that sister over in Omaha," Pop-Pop reminded her.

"The sister who never visits? The sister who only calls on Christmas and when she needs money?" Nana shook her head, tone heavy with disapproval. "You really think she's gonna stir herself from her trailer to do anythin' about that farm?"

"Dunno. But if Jim's got a will, it'll spell everythin' out. Dependin' on what's in there, sister might get it whether she wants it or not."

"And if he doesn't have one?"

"County gets it, I guess. We'll just have to wait until the damned lawyers get around to settlin' everythin' and see what happens then."

"That could take weeks. Months."

"Could," Pop-Pop grunted.

"And until then?" Nana asked him. "Who's gonna keep things up?"

"Not much to keep up anymore," Pop-Pop told her. "Cows're mostly gone—I can look after the few that are left. Bull'll be gone soon, too, so that's just leaves the house. Figure we lock it up and let it sit until everythin' settles out."

Nana nodded again, face thoughtful, fork pushing food around her plate. "Jim's gonna need to be buried. Funerals are expensive. Sister might not be able to cover it."

"Sister a-his is a deadbeat," Pop-Pop grunted. "Most days she ain't got two pennies to rub together. And if she did, she probably wouldn't spend 'em on Jim."

"Clem," Nana scolded.

"'S'truth, Evie, and ya know it."

Nana's silence spoke volumes. Made her thoughts on the subject clear.

"Got a bit put aside," Pop-Pop relented. "We can probably help 'er out. Man deserves a proper burial, not some cut-rate pine box buried under a bunch-a weeds in the corner of some forgotten cemetery."

"That's dark, Clem. Even for you."

"Dark day, Evie," Pop-Pop sighed. "Lost a good friend today. An *old* friend. Seen things..." Another sigh, eyes drifting to Casey. "Seen things the last few days I'd rather I hadn't."

Casey nodded, agreeing, as Nana reached over and patted his hand.

Curled her fingers around his, giving it a gentle squeeze.

***

That night, Casey dreamed again. A nightmare that started like the last one: with him sitting, playing with his dinosaurs on the bedroom floor.

He snuck a look out the window, expecting fire and the Bimiangus, blinked in surprise at finding neither and decided this dream was all right.

He liked dreams that involved playing with toys, just as long as the crazy bulls stayed away. And nothing was on fire.

He growled fiercely, smashing the T-Rex and the stegosaurus together. Letting them go at it for a while—snarling and biting as they vied for world domination. Grimaced and put them down, belatedly realizing they were covered in some kind of sticky goo.

Jam probably. Or peanut butter. Sometimes he took them down to the kitchen and played with them at lunch.

He wiped his hands on his pajama bottoms, smearing something red and wet into the fabric. Turned them over and found a suspicious layer of something red and gooey coating the entirety of his palms.

Red-red, not jelly red. No way that was strawberry preserves.

A blob of it peeled away, plopping wetly to the floor.

Casey poked at it, watching the fallen blob wiggle like gelatin. Picked at a strip clinging between his fingers, grimacing at the feel of it peeling away.

Wet and slimy. Like snot, or worse.

A shiver and Casey tossed it over his shoulder, picking at another spot. Spat on his palms and rubbed them together, scrubbing his hands against his pajama bottoms after to wipe away every last bit of that sticky slime goo.

"Gross. Gross-gross-gross," he mumbled, totally creeped out.

Didn't know where all that sticky stuff had come from, but it definitely wasn't peanut butter and jelly sandwich. In fact, he didn't think it was food at all.

A last swipe of his hands and he picked up the dinosaurs, cleaning them as best he could. Resumed the epic battle for Jurassic domination when they stopped feeling sticky, plastic bodies crashing together with much growling, and biting, and gnashing of sharp, plastic teeth.

"Rawwrr!" Casey cried, slamming the dinosaurs together. Blinking in surprise when they disintegrated in his hands. Plastic turning to burnt skin in an instant, sticky blood pouring across Casey's hands.

He screamed and threw the toys' remains away from him. Scooted backward, leaving a trail of wet handprints behind him as he paddled across the room on his butt. Fetched up against the toy box and stared in horror at the lumps of putrid flesh lying on the floorboards, fluids leaking from two tiny, dinosaur bodies, trickling in stinking streams across the floor.

Bubbled and rippled as it trickled and flowed. Fat maggots squirming beneath the surface, wriggling free to crawl in an inching torrent, heading straight for Casey, crammed up against that toy box beneath the window.

"No-no-no-no-no," he breathed, head whipping back and forth.

He clawed his way up onto the toy box, tucking his legs under him as he perched on top. Scooted as far away from the maggot hoard as possible, pressing his back against the window, hands wrapping around the toy box lid's edge.

Something squished beneath Casey's fingers, making him freeze up tight. He lifted his hand and turned it over, staring in horror at the T-Rex head stuck to his palm.

"AAAAHHHHH!"

He swiped one hand against the other, palms scraping, desperate to clear the clinging T-Rex head off. Popped it loose after a few seconds of effort, sending it sailing across the room—right *across* the small sea of maggots—to the stand-up mirror sitting in one corner.

The T-Rex head hit the glass, splatting wetly, leaving a bloody smear. Dropped to the floor and rolled over, stared accusingly with its dead doll's eyes.

The maggots reached it a few seconds later, an ocean of corpse-white army ants washing over the T-Rex's head. Crunching and munching as they swarmed around it, leaving a tiny, bone T-Rex skull behind when they moved on.

Casey screamed, voice filled with terror. "Nana! Pop-Pop! Help!" he yelled as the maggots reached the bottom of the toy chest, multiplying ten-fold as they inched up the side.

An ocean of them covered the floorboards now, consuming every last thing in that room.

Except the toy box, and Casey—an island in that sea of corpse-eating worms. An island now surrounded, leaving Casey, "Trapped," he whispered, looking around him in horror. "Nowhere to go."

Except the window, and that led outside.

Casey turned his head, considering it, and the thirty-foot drop on the other side. Far enough for someone stupid or desperate enough to jump out of it and break a leg or two. Possibly worse.

Then again, the alternative wasn't necessarily that much better. Sitting here, waiting for the maggots to wash over him and gobble him up like that T-Rex head wasn't exactly Casey's idea of a good time.

He grabbed at the sash, grunting as he heaved with all his might. But the window—swollen with moisture—stubbornly resisted, refusing to open.

"No-no-no-no-no," Casey screamed, tugging as hard as he could. "Open, you stupid thing!"

He beat at it, thinking to break the glass, but the panes were indestructible—impervious to his fists.

"Help!" he screamed, hysterical now, completely at the end of his rope. "Help me! Somebody get me out!"

"*Moo*?" A familiar voice called from the darkness outside. "*Moo-haroo*?"

"No. No, not you. You're gone. You're supposed to be gone."

Pop-Pop promised. Pop-Pop swore he'd make it dead.

"How can you not be gone?"

A chattering came from somewhere behind him—the sound of a hundred-thousand teeny-tiny teeth grinding together. Casey swiped at his feet, screaming as something tickled at his toes. Spread across his feet, crawling its way up his ankles to his pajama pants, tiny teeth ticking and clicking as they ate their way to his brains.

The last thing Casey heard before the tickling teeth filled his ears was the sound of the Bimiangus *mooing*. Calling to him through the window, wondering what was the matter.

\*\*\*

Casey woke screaming, batting at his arms and legs. Convinced he was covered in icky, fat maggots slowly eating him to death.

But there were no maggots on him when he finally calmed down enough to check. Nor in the bed, either. On the floor, or anywhere else in that room. Just a twisted bedsheet—which, to be fair, was white and therefore easily confused with maggots—and two plastic dinosaurs sitting innocently in the middle of the floor.

"Safe," he gasped, heart racing. "Just a nightmare."

He flopped back onto the mattress, hammering heart, doing the rumba in his chest. Waves of relief washing over him, drowning out the fear. A deep breath as he unwound the bed sheet, crawled to the end of his bed and hung his head over, checking the area beneath for pasty wrigglers.

Nothing. Not a single fat maggot in sight. No signs of blood or goo, either. Just dust bunnies, a shriveled-up spider, and a single discarded sock.

A dream. Just a dream. The blood, the maggots, all of it.

Outside, the storm raged, rain rattling against the bedroom window—a staccato pecking at the glass—and inside, darkness. Dark and scary, especially after that dream.

Casey shivered, eying the shadows in every corner, the bedroom turned creepy and sinister by their presence. Spotted the dinosaurs on the floor and scooped them up, braving the rain outside the window long enough to open the sash and the screen behind it and dump the toys in the yard.

No more dinosaurs. Not ever again.

Casey closed the screen and the window after, wiping raindrops from his hands. "Phew. Glad that's taken care of. Now back to—"

*Thump-thump-thump.*

Casey froze, turning wide eyes toward the bedroom door. "Hello?"

*Thump-thump-thump* from downstairs. Something bumping up against the wall of the house.

"It's just a shutter," Casey told himself. "Just a shutter that's come loose blowing in the wind."

A perfectly plausible explanation. Too bad Casey didn't quite believe it.

"Nana?" he called as the *thumping* continued. "Pop-Pop? You awake?"

Silence from the bedroom down the hall. His grandparents slipping sleeping.

No help coming from Nana and Pop-Pop, then.

*Thump-thump-thump.*

"Right. I'm just gonna go back to bed now," Casey said, creeping across the floor.

*Thump-thump-thump. Thump-thump-thump. Thud.*

"Just a loose shutter. It's just a loose shutter."

*Thud-thud-thud.*

Definitely coming from downstairs. The kitchen, maybe. Someone getting a midnight snack.

*Thud-thud-thud.*

"Nana? Pop-Pop? Is that you?" Casey called.

No answer, but that didn't necessarily mean anything. Nana and Pop-Pop were both hard of hearing. Especially with their hearing aids out.

Casey considered his bed and the safety of its covers, crept the other way—toward the cracked-open bedroom door—and peered down the night-dark hall to his grandparents' bedroom at the opposite end.

Found the door down there shut tight, Nana and Pop-Pop sleeping blissfully while their scaredy-cat grandson worried about some ominous sound coming from the kitchen.

"It's nothing," Casey told himself.

*Thud-thud-thud.*

Louder this time. Definitely louder. Or maybe it was just his imagination.

Casey thought about going downstairs to investigate, and prove he wasn't a complete chicken. But as he stood there, trying to work up the courage, the *thudding* suddenly stopped, leaving the house incredibly quiet.

Very, very still.

Ten seconds that silence lasted before another *thud* came—loud, heavy, make the whole house rattle—followed by a splintering crash.

"What—What—What—?" Casey stammered, staring wide-eyed at the stairs. "Who—Who—Who—?" He backed away from the door as footsteps came from below. Someone or some*thing* moving about the kitchen, broken glass crunching, chairs scraping and tipping over as those footsteps crossed the linoleum and stepped onto the living room's hardwood floors.

The sound of *huffling* and *whuffling* moving with them as something, some beast, some awful hound from hell, scuffed across Nana's carefully maintained flooring, moaning and groaning as it invaded his grandparent's house.

Casey slammed the bedroom door and raced across his room, threw himself at the bed and burrowed under the covers, pulling everything—sheets, blanket, even the pillow—over his head. Lay there, shivering, as the *thumping* and *banging* continued, some obviously heavy body knocking things over, sharp-edged feet scuffing across the hardwood floors, clattering harshly as they mounted the stairs.

"No," Casey whispered. "No, please. Go 'way."

"*Moo,*" the Bimiangus called, stairs creaking beneath him.

Casey pressed his hands to his mouth, sobbing silently. Curled into a ball and hugged his legs to his chest. "Please go away-Please go away-Please go away."

"*Moo!*" the Bimiangus bellowed, mounting another step. "*Moo-haroo!*"

"Nana?" Casey called, louder this time, hoping she would hear. "Nana?!"

Nothing—not one peep from that other bedroom. No one coming to save him. For all intents and purposes, it was just Casey, the darkness and that bull.

*Thunk-thunk-drag, thunk-thunk-drag*—that was the sound of the Bimiangus climbing those old, wooden stairs. The heavy tread of bovine feet providing an ominous accompaniment to the squishy, wet, slopping sound of the dangling shreds of the bull's burnt hide. Flayed skin slapping, dragging wetly across the treads.

"Oh geez-oh geez-oh geez," Casey whispered, hyperventilating now.

The *thunking* and *dragging* reached the top of the stairs, stopped and went quiet a while. A clatter of cloven hooves as the Bimiangus turned, and dragging turned to slithering as the bull clomped its way to Casey's bedroom door.

"*Moo?*" it called to Casey, wondering why he was hiding.

A thump as it reached the door, clattering to a halt outside. "*Moo-haroo,*" the Bimiangus moaned. "*Moo-moo-haroo!*" it greeted him, bovine sounds Casey's brain translated as 'Let me in, little boy, so I can eat the skin off your face'. It thumped against the door making the entire thing jump. Butted at it with its head and shoulders, backed up and hit it hard.

*How are Nana and Pop-Pop not hearing this?* Casey wondered, door creaking as the latch popped open. *How can anyone sleep through all this noise?*

A snort as the Bimiangus butted the door open, pushing it wide with its oversized snout. A *whuff* as it scented the air, searching for Casey, followed by the *thump-thump-slide* of it crossing the room. Approaching the bed.

"Oh god-Oh god-Oh god."

Casey burrowed deeper into the bed sheets, stuffing his fist in his mouth to stop himself from shrieking. Nostrils flaring, cheeks puffing and deflating as he sipped panicked breaths. Hidden as he was, he couldn't actually *see* the bull, but somehow that actually made things worse. So, he peeled the sheet back the tiniest bit, scanning the room. Spotted green eyes reflecting off the stand-up mirror in the corner. A hulking shadow standing at the end of his bed.

"*Moo*," it *lowed*, bovine voice sounding mournful in the dark.

"I'm going to eat you," that keening call meant. "I'm going to munch on your toes, and snuffle at your guts. Burrow my tongue into your eyes and slurp your brains from your skull."

Casey puffed around his fist even harder, almost choking as he sucked saliva down his throat.

"*Moo*?" The Bimiangus prodded at the bed, snuffling it with his nose. Hot breath speckling the cream-colored sheets with crimson showers, adding tiny, red polka dots to the blanket's pattern of flowers. "*Moo-haroo?*" it called, mounting the bed, climbing up almost daintily, one bovine leg at a time.

The bed creaked alarmingly, swayed and rocked from side-to-side. Casey clung to it, half expecting to be pitched right over and sent tumbling across the floor. Moaned as a warm wetness soaked through the bedding, sticking it to his side.

"No. Oh, no-no-no-no-no," Casey whimpered, scrambling away, smashing his body against the headboard because that was as far away as he could get. Couldn't actually *leave* the bed now, not with the Bimiangus atop it, pinning the sheets tight. And with the bull looming over him—hogging the bed never designed for a creature of his weight and girth—he had his hands full just trying to avoid getting crushed by it. Stomped to death by those sharp-edged hooves.

Casey lowered the sheets, sneaking a look at it. Staring in horror at entrails spilling wetly on the bedding, hanging in shreaded tubes from the bull's burst open gut. Muscles and fat, a red and white tangle, all wrapped up with the loose folds of dragging, crispy skin.

"This isn't happening. This can't be happening," he whispered as the bull's head came 'round, glowing, toxic eyes locking onto his face.

"*Moo!*" it greeted him cheerily, cloven hoofs shifting, balancing delicately atop that bed.

Blood pattered from its shredded middle, running in sticky streaks down its sides. A slab of flesh peeled away from its back and plopped down beside its foot. Everything soaking now. Covered in blood and ichor. The blanket, the sheets, the mattress and Casey—all of them sharing the Bimiangus' leavings. The rank odor of gasoline and corruption, farts, and chemicals, and fermented grass that drifted around it, mixing with that smell of blood-blood-blood.

Casey choked on it, stomach heaving, everything he'd eaten for dinner demanding to be let out. He turned his head, squiggling as far as the tight sheets would allow. Hung his head over the side of the bed and puked his guts out. Half-digested meat and vegetables, that chocolate cake he'd had for dessert, everything Casey had eaten for breakfast, lunch and dinner spewing out in one monstrous, record-setting hurl.

"*Moo?*" the bull called, sounding concerned. It nipped at the blankets, pulling them aside. Studied Casey a moment—head tilting, poisoned eyes blinking—circled once and flopped down, heaving a wet sigh.

Casey lay there stiffly, staring wide-eyed at the ceiling—two tons of bovine flesh pressing up against him, spooning with him like a lover in the dark.

Heat baked off it—rancid, stinking, a blast furnace burning just beneath its skin. Blood leaked everywhere, a constant seepage that drenched Casey, sticking his pajamas to his body, his hair to the bed.

A *whuffle* and the Bimiangus leaned over, nuzzling at his face. Muttering, "*Moo-moo-moo,*" so gently, so tenderly as it unfurled its slimy, pink length of tongue and licked delicately at Casey's face.

"Uhhhh. Uhhhh," Casey whimpered, trembling. Overwhelmed with disgust. Hating the feel of the thing, the smell of the thing, the sticky strings of spittle that lapping tongue left behind.

A snort of hot breath sprayed blood and yellow-green snot, adding a second layer of slime to the one already coating Casey's face. But the tongue retreated, mercifully, and the glowing-eyed head turned away as the Bimiangus wriggled, burrowing under the covers to snuggle close. Sniffed at Casey, a *whuffling* like a mother inspecting her kittens, and proceeded to clean him. Licking Casey from head to toe.

That cleaning was horrible—the worst thing Casey was forced to endure in all of his ten years on this earth. But he lay there and took it, having no other choice—no one to come save him, no way to get out. Shivered and quivered with his eyes closed and his hands clenched into fists at his side until the licking slowed and finally stopped. Lay there trembling, while the Bimiangus snuffled at him, checking its work. Heaved another snotty, bloody sigh and pressed its putrid body against him, cuddling Casey like a teddy bear.

"*Moo,*" it groaned, taking a last swipe at Casey's face. "*Moo-haroo,*" the Bimiangus mumbled sleepily, rank, rancid breath puffing across Casey's face.

A last slimy tickle, flailing at Casey's cheek, and the bull tucked up tightly, pillowing its burnt head on its legs. Closed its eyes and drifted to sleep, dreaming whatever terrible dreams a monster like it imagined.

# TEN

CASEY DIDN'T SLEEP a wink that night—no way, no how, not with the Bimiangus sleeping close by. The blood, and intestines, and other loose body parts turning the bed into a quagmire of disgustingness. The bull itself snoring like a cranky old motor, farting non-stop.

Hour after hour, he endured the stink of it, the feel of it, the noise of that half-dead thing pressing against his side. The clock ticking endless beside him—a ratcheting, clacking sound keeping time with the thumping heart in Casey's chest. And all the while, one thought—just one—running endlessly through his mind: What happens when it wakes again? What will the Bimiangus do to me when it wakes up?

Surprisingly, it was nothing. Well, not nothing-nothing, but it didn't kill him, which Casey supposed was a plus. Dawn broke, a faint light coloring the sky outside his window, and the Bimiangus woke with it. Snorted and farted wetly as it gathered its legs under it and stood.

Blinked at Casey, as if surprised to find him lying there, sharing that gore stained bed. Yawned, and stretched, and turned around, head dipping to give Casey one last parting lick before it clattered to the floor, and *thump-thump-slid* across the room.

Down the stairs. Through the kitchen. Hooves *clomping* as it exited out the kitchen door.

Casey lay very still through all of it, shoulders hitching with barely suppressed sobs. Curled up tight and wrapped his arms around his shins as the sobs turned to shivers, tears bursting free, rolling in fat droplets down his face.

Wasn't sure how long he stayed that way, but eventually the shivers ended, the sobs and tears ran out. The door to his grandparents' bedroom opened soon after, Nana's soft voice muttering something about 'thoughtless people dragging mud all over her nice clean floors' as she walked down the stairs, *tsking* when she reached the rooms below.

"Nana," Casey called, broken voice a croaking whisper. "Nana," he tried again, as she bustled about below, righting the chairs in the kitchen, cleaning up the mud, and blood, and manure from the floors.

Casey climbed from the bed as the pots and pans appeared—Nana clattering and clanging as she started cooking. Climbed atop the toy box and looked outside.

Nothing. No sign at all of the Bimiangus. Just an empty pasture and the long, double line of fencing. Grass everywhere, surrounding Mr. Perkins' red-sided barn.

Wreckage in his room, though. Blood everywhere, mud everywhere, stinking lumps of manure dotting the hoof prints marking the bull's path.

Bits of sloughed-off skin, here and there, which was disgusting. A coil of intestines lying on the floor.

For some reason that made him giggle, shoulders twitching as he clapped his hands to his mouth.

Not right, laughing about intestines after spending a night in bed with a mostly-dead bull. Not right laughing about *any* of this, especially with poor Mr. Perkins dead.

A last, hitching giggle and Casey forced the laughter down. Stuffing it deep, deep inside him and hoped it wouldn't come back out.

Crazy people laughed about things like rotting bulls and murder. Spending the night with zombified livestock.

Casey didn't want to be crazy. He just wanted to get off this farm.

He pushed away from the toy chest, heading for the door, tugging idly at the ichor-encrusted pajama bottoms sticking wetly to his legs. Thumps from the bedroom across the ball meant Pop-Pop was up and moving around. Casey thought about waiting and talking to Nana and Pop-Pop together, but figured Nana on her own would be more sympathetic. More likely to send him home right away.

So, he descended the stairs, treads tacky and slightly slippery beneath his feet. Stepped across the pool of blood at the bottom, and shambled over to the kitchen, calling, "Nana?" in a wavering 'I-need-help' voice.

Nana glanced over her shoulder as he stepped into the kitchen, scooping pancakes from a skillet that she piled on a plate. "Breakfast is just about ready, honey. Be a dear and grab the orange juice from the fridge."

"Nana?" Casey slid a step closer, staring at her face. "Nana?"

"Land's sakes, Casey! What is it with you this morning?" Nana sighed in exasperation, side-stepping to the cabinet to pull three juice glasses down. "Nana-Nana-Nana," she said, thumping the glasses on the table without looking. "Sound like some kind of parrot!"

"Nana," Casey called, lips trembling, body starting to shake. "Nana, I had a bad dream."

It wasn't a dream, but how else could he explain it? The truth sounded crazy, and he was trying to *pretend* he was normal. A scared kid who really, truly just wanted to go home.

"Aww, Casey dear," Nana said, in her softest, gentlest voice. "It's all right." She turned plate in hand, offering a grandmotherly smile. Frowned and looked him up and down, head tilting to one side. "Casey. Have you been outside playing in the mud?"

Casey shook his head, lips quivering as an aching began. A throbbing deep inside his head.

Nana leaned down, face wrinkling in concern. Set the pancake plate aside as she waved Casey close. "Casey dear," she said, gnarled hands settling on his shoulders. "What's wrong with your eyes?"

# ABOUT THE AUTHOR

BORN AND RAISED in the maple-syrup wilds of New England, J.B. Rockwell once chased dreams of being the next Indiana Jones, until an unforeseen series of twists and turns (involving cats, a marriage, and a SCUBA certification, amongst other things) led her to a career in IT. In her spare time, she scribbles nonsense that sometimes turn into stories, and has successfully authored three novels in the *Serengeti* series from Severed Press (*Serengeti, Dark and Stars,* and *Hecate*), as well as an all new, stand-alone novel, *Forgotten Stars & Distant Seas,* forthcoming from Severed Press in late 2020.

www.ingramcontent.com/pod-product-compliance
Lightning Source LLC
Chambersburg PA
CBHW020316150626
46552CB00022B/2901